RUM COUNTRY

J WILLIAM

Copyright ©2018 J William All rights reserved.

All Rights Reserved.

No part of this publication may be reproduced, distributed, or transmitted in any form or by any means, including photocopying, recording, electronic, or mechanical methods, without the prior written permission of the publisher, except in the case of brief quotations embodied in critical reviews and certain other non-commercial uses permitted by copyright law.

Neither the publisher nor author will be held responsible for any inaccuracies.

ISBN: 978-1-720189-54-1

For the girl who can do anything.

Dear Reader,

Some of you may find the spelling is not what you are used to. The story is written using British English, and has characters who are American, Australian, and British, and as such, their thoughts and speaking parts will be in their native language; which might not be words you are familiar with, but they are not errors. I hope you enjoy the variety.

Table of Contents

INTRODUCTION: WAITING..11

CHAPTER 1: BILLY..15

CHAPTER 2: THE TUNNEL..26

CHAPTER 3: THE CONTAINER..29

CHAPTER 4: THE MAP 33

CHAPTER 5: FLIGHT...37

CHAPTER 6: AMY 40

CHAPTER 7: ISSY 43

CHAPTER 8: GETTING TO KNOW YOU..47

CHAPTER 9: ARRIVAL 49

CHAPTER 10: SUSPICION..53

CHAPTER 11: THE APARTMENTS 55

CHAPTER 12: HORSES AT DAWN 59

CHAPTER 13: THE COMPASS..65

CHAPTER 14: THE SPLIT 68

CHAPTER 15: THE COVE 70

CHAPTER 16: OISTINS 75

CHAPTER 17: DRINKING 94

CHAPTER 18: INSOMNIA 102

CHAPTER 19: THE SEDUCTION 103

CHAPTER 20: THE CHASE 106

CHAPTER 21: COMPANY 116

CHAPTER 22: TRAPPED 127

CHAPTER 23: THE CAVE 135

CHAPTER 24: DARKNESS 147

CHAPTER 25: LIGHT 156

CHAPTER 26: JUNGLE 161

CHAPTER 27: SANCTUARY 166

CHAPTER 28: SUPPER 171

CHAPTER 29: THE WATCHMAN 178

CHAPTER 30: RUN 183

CHAPTER 31: TAXI DRIVER *188*

CHAPTER 32: DECISION *190*

CHAPTER 33: HORIZON *193*

A Few Words *194*

INTRODUCTION: WAITING

Jake stared out at the cobbled street, watching the few people brave enough to face the abysmal weather scurrying along outside.

It was as bad as he'd seen it.

The rain seemed to be travelling sideways straight in to the pane of glass he was looking through, as if it was holding it in place.

He felt trapped.

When he'd moved to Bristol a year and a half ago, he had imagined embarking on a high-flying career.

He liked the idea of being a lawyer and working in one of the big Georgian office buildings in Queen Square, it was probably his favourite daydream.

Working in finance had been a fleeting goal too, and advertising, basically he'd considered anything that would give him a life where he could afford a house, a car, and plenty of holidays.

Everything seemed so expensive these days.

But he hadn't made a lot of progress in the 'dream career' department and had been working in a restaurant for most of his time.

Jake hadn't meant to drift, but there had been so much going on compared to where he'd grown up in Falmouth, that it had been easy.

His favourite haunt was King Street, and in particular a pub called the Llandoger Trow, where he was currently sitting, sipping his lager.

He had stumbled across its whitewash exterior and thick, black timber beams on a night out. The ancient bar and lounge areas had radiated with adventures past and he knew he could happily get lost in there.

The pub dated back to 1664 and was supposedly the spot author Daniel Defoe had met sailor Alexander Selkirk, a man who had lived as a castaway for four years on a remote island in the Caribbean, after his ship abandoned him.

The story went that Defoe then based the book Robinson Crusoe on Selkirk's experiences.

It was also said pirates had regularly spent time in the pub, using secret passages underneath the building to transport cargo from the docks undetected.

Jake loved all the history and whenever he visited he would imagine how it must have been back in Defoe's time when the pub was full of pirates, wondering what secret conversations were had and what happened to those that had been involved in them.

It didn't take him long to pick up the stories of the area, the docks, and the more notorious pirates from the region.

He retold them over and over to his friends, work colleagues, and anyone who would listen.

On the whole, Jake was enjoying life. He lived in a small but cosy studio apartment near the centre of the city, he didn't hate his work, and he loved Bristol.

But the nagging voice in his head wouldn't go away.

He knew deep down he wanted something different, unfortunately he had no idea what that was or how to go about getting it.

"I'll get back on the job hunt after Billy's gone," he told himself, and continued to recall some of the better pirate stories he'd heard that he could tell his friend when he arrived.

* * *

Jake had met Billy on a ski trip a couple of years earlier. They had looked after a German family in a chalet, taking turns to cook and clean, then skiing, snowboarding, and drinking as much as they could in between.

Originally from Ithaca, Billy now lived in New York. He was a total Anglophile and when he'd first met Jake many hours had been spent comparing upbringings and cultural differences. He'd been glued to every detail about life in England.

Now that Billy was actually going to be in the land he was so obsessed with, Jake wanted to impress him with as much interesting history, and as many typically British things to see and do as he could.

Last year, Jake had made the trip to New York. It had been his first time in America, and he had absolutely loved it.

The buildings, the people, the bars, everything had been so big, loud, and bright, and he hoped the south-west of England could live up to Billy's expectations and be as entertaining for him as New York had been for Jake.

When he'd visited, the pair had picked up where they'd left off, and any doubt over whether they were really friends or whether they'd just connected on a one-off holiday vanished.

Billy was due in around six p.m. at Heathrow, then he was getting the train to Temple Meads, and a taxi to the Trow, where Jake was waiting for him.

Because it was a Sunday Jake hoped it wouldn't be too busy by the evening. Then they could find a quiet table and catch up properly.

He took another sip of his lager and held it up to the weather as if saying cheers to the rain, then sat back waiting for Billy's arrival.

CHAPTER 1: BILLY

The weather refused to let up.

Jake hoped the wind, rain, lightning, cats, dogs, and whatever-the-hell else kept falling from the sky wouldn't cause too much delay to Billy's flight.

He was beginning to wish they'd planned a trip somewhere warmer.

The plan was to hang out in the city for a few days, see the sights—and the pubs—then head to the coast so Billy could see where Jake was from. He had hoped they could go out on his dad's boat, and maybe do some surfing too.

Still, it would be good to see Billy, and two weeks without work would be a welcome change, even if most of it would be spent within a few miles of his flat.

"Oi! We're next. We ordered two Tributes over here ten minutes ago," a man with an unkempt white moustache moaned to the barman loudly, snapping Jake from his daydream.

The pub was full, but subdued. The festivities of Friday and Saturday night, when there had been live Jazz at the Duke opposite and swarms of people covering all the benches on the cobbles outside had now died down as the prospect of Monday morning work loomed.

Jake's mood, however, was in the ascendency.

His eyes kept catching on the hands of the wall-clock, willing them to turn faster so his friend would arrive, and they could really get on it.

As ten o'clock approached Billy finally walked through the door, sheets of water falling off his long, black coat and instantly creating puddles on the floor.

"Mate! I was worried your flight had been cancelled because of the storm," Jake said, giving his friend a hug.

"Yeh, we got lucky. The pilot said we managed to find a gap or something, and anyway, I made it. Man, I need a beer. What have we got?"

"On it," Jake said, walking over to the bar. "Two lagers and two dark rums, please."

The barman reached up to the top shelf and took down a half-full bottle of

Kraken. "Doubles?"

Jake nodded.

He watched as the barman poured two generous measures, added ice, and handed the glasses over before reaching for two pint glasses.

Jake took the spirits back to the table. "Try this. Should warm you up a bit."

"Cheers," Billy said, taking a sip. "Damn, that's good. Haven't tried that one before."

Jake fetched the other two drinks and sat down opposite.

"Well, you wanted authentic England." He laughed, nodding once again to the weather, which, if anything, had gotten worse.

"Cheers." They clinked glasses and then Billy proceeded to tell Jake about his journey, the crazy people who had been on his flight, and what was happening back home.

The initial awkwardness from not seeing each other for a while vanished quickly.

Aside from one small but lively group a couple of tables over, and a few other more quiet couples, Jake had been right. It had been a quiet night and as closing approached people began to leave, even before they were asked.

Jake saw the barman go over to the table of stragglers one over from them, three young lads and two girls.

"How about a lock-in mate?" one of the group piped up, seeing him heading towards them.

"Not tonight, yeh. Come on, I just want to lock-up and go home."

"Just a couple more drinks and we'll push out," said one of the lads. "Please, sir, can I have some more?" Putting his hands together pretending to beg and getting a laugh from his mates.

He was the loudest and looked like he'd had the most to drink.

The two girls were giggling and whispering something to each other.

Then Jake realised they were looking over towards their table.

The blonde got up and walked over to the bar, leaning her elbows on the counter, and occasionally glancing in Billy's direction.

She had on a strappy top and mini-skirt, and Jake couldn't help thinking that she must have been absolutely freezing wearing so little in this weather.

"Just a couple more and I promise we'll leave after that. It's grim outside, give us another hour and hopefully it'll have passed, and then we won't get absolutely soaked on the way home," she said, trying to sound as reasonable as she could.

The barman sighed, sensing the protests that would inevitably follow. "Sorry. I've got rules to follow I'm afraid. You've got time for one more, then that's your lot. What'll it be?" he added quickly, hoping to appease the rabble in front of him.

"Are you lads having one more too?" he asked, gesturing to Jake and Billy.

The blonde, again, looked over in their direction.

"Come on, I'll buy you a drink. What you having?" She smiled at Billy.

Jake couldn't quite make out her accent, or the accent of anyone else in her group, but he was pretty sure they weren't from the area.

"Sure, why not?" Billy said, grinning back. "We'll have two rums, please."

The loudest lad, who'd called for the lock-in bristled as he saw his plan disintegrate in front of him.

He didn't seem to like either his girlfriend, or a girl he'd been trying to get friendly with, flirting with some randoms, but he more importantly he wanted the final drink on offer, so he bit his tongue.

His mood had visibly darkened, and he didn't take his eyes off the girl at the bar, especially when she sauntered over to personally deliver the drinks to her new friends.

In the minutes that followed, Jake uneasily watched events unfold.

Billy clearly thought his luck was in with the blonde girl, who he'd discovered was called Chloe, and couldn't have been happier. Within hours of being in England, he was getting chatted up.

Chloe was equally pleased with this development. She'd been delighted to find out Billy was from New York and was enjoying the attention he was lavishing on her.

The only person who was put out was the lad, who Jake had overheard was called Steve, and both Billy and Chloe were oblivious to, or were pretending to ignore, the fact he had been scowling relentlessly at them in the background ever since Chloe had sat down.

"Yeh, it gets super cold in the winter. Because everything is in a grid the wind picks up and goes right through you. It's a great city though. There's always stuff going on," Billy said, finishing his answer to Chloe's latest round of questions about New York.

His strong American accent rang out around the now empty bar and added to Steve's growing hatred of Billy, and by association, Jake too.

"I've never been but I've always wanted to go, maybe I can come and visit?" she said, leaning in closer as she said it.

Steve couldn't take anymore.

"Fuck this, I'm taking a slash and we're getting out of this shit-hole," he declared loudly, smashing over a chair as he bowled out of the room towards the bathroom.

The barman went over to their table and started to collect the last of the glasses, asking the three still sitting there to start getting their things together as he was closing up.

He then came over to Jake and Billy's table. "Come on, guys, time to go."

"No worries, thanks for letting us stay a bit."

"I'm just going to the loo then let's make a move," he said to Billy, before getting up and heading towards the bathrooms.

"They regulars?" he asked the barman as they walked from the table towards the bar together.

"Nope. Never seen them in here before. I've got my eye on that one though." The barman nodded towards the bathroom, then carried on cleaning up.

As Jake approached the door to the men's toilet, he began to worry he'd made a mistake in following the drunk in to the toilets.

Shit, I should have waited, he thought, slowly pushing the door open and wondering what state he'd find Steve in. He'd seemed pretty smashed and definitely looked like he could handle himself.

Jake, by contrast, had messy brown almost blond hair, bright blue eyes, clean-shaven, and regularly got told by his mum and the elderly regulars to their family café that he had a kind face.

Even the tattoos he'd gotten when he was still in his late teens after one too many cheek pinches had done little to roughen up his appearance. Instead, he'd just been labelled a hipster.

On his left arm Jake had a sailor's knot, which wrapped a few times around his wrist, and on his right arm he had a tattoo of his dad's boat, the sails reaching up his forearm and the name of the boat, Adelaide, inked in to the side of the vessel in italic typography.

Jake was certain his appearance wasn't going to worry Steve and he was not relishing a confrontation. He prayed that Steve had simply been sick on himself and fallen asleep or had suddenly sobered up and stopped acting like such a twat.

Jake took a deep breath and stepped in to the men's toilet slowly. No one was there.

"Fuck, where is he?" Jake wondered out loud. He unbuttoned his fly and kept half an eye over his shoulder.

When he'd finished, he washed his hands then quickly exited the toilet, suddenly feeling uneasy about Steve's absence.

He imagined the guy rampaging around the pub off-limits, trashing the place.

Just as he had decided to tell the barman Steve was missing he received a blow to the side of his body that smashed him into the wall and caused him to tumble down the first few stairs leading to the cellar.

As he tumbled, random thoughts flooded his head about ghosts he'd been told lived in the basement of the Trow and throughout the creaking building. Allegedly, there were fifteen of them knocking about the place, visiting with varying regularity.

He panicked at the prospect of getting trapped down there in the dark, with this angry drunk and a load of dead sailors to keep him company.

Jake struggled to his feet, looked up and saw Steve at the top of the stairs towering over him. Instinctively, he put a foot behind him and edged slowly downwards in the direction he least wanted to go.

"You and your yank friend don't look so smug, now do you?" Steve slurred.

Jake didn't feel it was the right time to point out Billy wasn't even with him right now. Instead, he increased his pace and kept feeling for the bottom step, hoping when he got there he'd find something in the cellar to put some distance, or barrier between himself and angry Steve.

After what seemed like an eternity of steps, he finally felt solid floor and turned to see where he could escape to.

He dashed to the far corner and watched Steve follow him down. Now he really was trapped.

Once Steve left the last step behind him, he seemed to lose focus for a moment, tipping over boxes, kicking barrels, and cursing loudly.

"Cunts!" he screamed, smashing his foot through an old storage box, then struggling to get it back out again.

Finally, he was free but still he struggled to regain his balance.

Jake noticed he now had an open bottle of what looked like vodka in his hand and was swaying. He didn't know if Steve had brought it with him or snatched it from somewhere in the pub, but he could clearly see the effect the amount he'd swigged was having.

Steve took a swing at another box and missed. He looked like he was torn between trying to trash the place, exacting some sort of revenge on Jake for some perceived slight, and simply drowning his sorrows.

"Mate, come on, let's get out of here and go back upstairs. We're leaving now, and we'll get out of your hair and you won't even see us again," Jake said, trying to sound as calm and reasonable as he could manage under the circumstances.

Steve looked up and edged closer towards him. In the dim cellar lights, Jake could see he was now massively pissed and glassy-eyed.

"Fuck off, I'll go whenever I FUCKING WANT TO!" he shouted, kicking a box hard to make a point. This one flew across the room and thudded against a side wall.

Steve staggered and swayed—and Jake saw his chance.

He figured as big as this guy was, he was also absolutely smashed. Sidling quickly behind him he put two hands on his shoulders and pushed Steve firmly towards the stairs. "Time to go, mate."

Steve spun around with the bottle, vodka spraying everywhere. It slipped from his grasp as his wrist connected clumsily with Jake's shoulder and smashed loudly to the ground.

They locked eyes for a split second, and Jake saw instantly he'd made a big mistake.

Steve was completely drunk, but he wasn't so drunk he couldn't still do a lot of damage.

A strong hand gripped Jake's throat and the arm attached to it forced him backward towards a rough stone wall.

Jake tried to shout for help, or to reason with the guy but his windpipe was being squashed and he could only croak and struggle for breath.

His back hit the wall behind him hard, and before he could feel any sense of relief at the grip releasing his neck, he saw Steve's broad shoulders twist and a punch fly at his face.

Jake shifted to the right as quickly as he could. The punch just caught his ear, but mainly connected with air and a bit of wall, judging by the painful expression on Steve's face.

As he repositioned his body for a second attempt, Jake spotted Billy's horrified face behind Steve in the background.

"HEY!" Billy yelled, speeding up as he reached the bottom of the stairs.

Steve turned quickly to find Billy full-on sprinting for him. He covered the ground between them in a flash and piled into Steve's midriff with his shoulder.

The momentum of the hit caused both of them to slam into Jake and all three hit the wall hard.

A sharp pain ran through Jake's body. He wasn't sure if it was his head, shoulder, or elbow that hurt, or maybe all of them.

As the three of them tried to stumble to their feet, Jake realised his elbow had actually gone through the wall behind him and was trapped. He pulled hard and dislodged himself, and more of the wall, painfully.

"I'm calling the cops," Billy said shakily, taking a step back and reaching for his phone, but never taking his eyes off Steve in front of him.

"What the fuck!? STEVE. What are you doing!" The voice belonged to Chloe who was at the top of the stairs with the rest her group, surveying the ridiculous scene.

"I'm out of here," she said as she turned away, disgusted. The other girl followed.

Steve's other mates looked like they wanted to leave too, but they had to deal with the mess that was Steve first. They slowly crept down the stairs towards Steve.

"What the… GET THE FUCK OUT! NOW!" the barman yelled, pushing through the small melee at the top of the stairs.

Steve's mates took him by the arm before he could kick-off again, and all of them went up the stairs, speeding up as they heard the barman's voice loudly say, "Police, please, yeh, I want to report an incident at the Llandoger Trow on King Street."

Jake breathed a sigh of relief as the bodies disappeared from the top of the stairs and slumped in a heap on the floor. "Thank God that's over," he said out loud.

The booze and adrenaline seemed to leave his body at the same time, and exhaustion kicked in.

He had no doubt where the pain was coming from now, his elbow was killing him.

"Wow, man, that was unreal," said Billy, crouching down next to his friend, looking at something on the wall behind Jake.

"Some intro to the UK. You plan all that just for me?" He laughed, slapping Jake's knee, still studying the wall.

"Yeh, I thought that's exactly what you'd need after your flight. You know, stretch your legs. I wasn't expecting the flying spear tackle, didn't know you had it in you." Jake laughed.

"I have absolutely no idea where that came from. I mean, I had to do something you were hiding in the corner like a frightened rabbit and there was a bit of distance to cover. I wanted to be fast and then by the time I got there, well, momentum just seemed to take over."

"You went all Hulk on him, it was hilarious. At least it would have been had I not been sandwiched between that idiot's back and the wall—my elbow is killing."

"Looks like you made quite a dent too," Billy said, pointing to the spot he'd been staring at for the last few minutes.

Jake turned to see there was now a hole in the wall, roughly a foot square. Through the hole was pitch black.

"What's behind there?" asked Billy.

"I have no idea. There are stories about a bunch of tunnels going to the docks that were blocked off years and years ago, I guess it could be one of those. This pub was a pirate hangout and they carried stuff to and from their ships. Stuff they didn't want the authorities to know about, I guess; illegal booze, guns, jewels. Stuff they'd robbed or were going to use to do some robbing basically."

"So, you're telling me we've just uncovered a secret tunnel that was used by pirates?"

"Um, yeh, it looks like it." He grinned, staring into the darkness beyond. "It gives me the creeps. There are loads of ghost stories about down here, and this pub, in general, actually. The Trow is supposedly Bristol's oldest pub, although loads of pubs claim that, don't they?"

Billy was intrigued. "That's so cool! We have to see what's behind there and, if it is a tunnel, where it goes."

"You're kidding me, right?" Jake said, looking again at the hole in the wall.

Billy walked over to the loose bricks around the edge of the hole and gave one of them a shove.

At first it didn't budge. Billy persisted and after three or four more shoves and a couple of kicks, the brick he was aiming for finally relented.

With a hollow clunk it hit the floor on the other side. "What the fuck are you doing?" Jake said shocked.

"Come on, man. Where's your sense of 'fuck it' gone? We've got a once in a lifetime chance to follow a real pirate trail—we've got to see where it goes. What's the worst that's going to happen? If we're quick, we'll be in and out before the barman's back. And if it does go somewhere... we've got a head-start." He grinned.

"You're crazy," was all Jake could reply but his smile gave him away.

"Ha! I knew it. Fucking hurry up and help me then. That barman will be back any minute."

"Asshole, you've been here five minutes and already you've got us into a fight and now we're trashing an historic landmark," he said, grinning.

"Hey, man. That girl came on to me. If you'd have taken care of business down here, I could have gotten lucky." Billy continued pulling on bricks. "I've nearly got this one, can you get that end?"

Jake moved over to give Billy a hand, with a brick now sticking out more than the others.

"Okay. On three. One, two, THREE," Billy shouted as they gave it everything.

The brick came free with some force and flew in to the hole, causing another sizeable collapse.

As they knocked through brick after brick, it became apparent to them that this section of the wall had been erected simply to make the entrance to the tunnel beyond invisible, rather than to block it off forever.

It meant Billy and Jake could quickly widen the gap sufficiently to squeeze through.

"You got a torch in this place?"

"Yeh, let me go and check. There should be one under the bar—I'll just go and ask the barman, shall I?" Jake said sarcastically.

"How about your phone then smart-ass? My battery's dying."

"Oh, yeh," Jake said, grinning, fumbling for the switch on his mobile. "Imagine if we find some ancient treasure that's worth millions." He laughed, holding the light towards the now significantly larger hole.

"Only one way to find out hurry up! Ladies first." Billy gestured towards the broken wall. "Take a look and see what's behind there."

Jake turned the phone-light to full beam, cleared a space in the rubble, and knelt down on the ground.

He put his hand clutching the phone through first, followed by his arm, head, torso, and then finally he used his arms to drag the rest of his body forward until his legs and feet dropped inside with the rest of him.

The smell of damp hit him first and it was perceptibly colder too. "Well, what can you see!?" Billy asked impatiently.

"I can't see a lot... there's just space. It looks like a cave. I'm shining the light over the ground to see if there's anything but nothing so far. Wait... there's a section furthest away that's darker. I can't tell but I think it goes on that way. Maybe this is the entrance to a tunnel. I'm coming out," he said, pulling back a little frantically.

"Fuck that. Stay there! Just take a breath and chill, I'm coming through."

Jake shone his makeshift light around behind him and saw Billy's head and torso squeezing through.

It was even more of a squeeze for Billy as he was significantly bigger, so Jake went over and grabbed his friend's top by the shoulders and heaved.

With a thud, Jake fell backwards, landing on his arse with Billy landing on top of him.

"That's the second time tonight you've flattened me, you fat fuck." Jake wheezed a laugh as they scrambled to their feet.

"I don't fancy going through there again," Billy said, looking at the hole behind him.

"I guess that only leaves one option." He grinned.

CHAPTER 2: THE TUNNEL

Jake went first, pointing the light in front of him with Billy following closely behind.

"It's big," said Billy. "Those pirates must have been moving a lot of stuff around."

The initial room felt vast but after Jake shined the light around two or three times, and their eyes had accustomed slightly to the darkness, they realised it was a lot smaller than they first thought.

"Measure it out in steps," Billy said. "One, two, three..."

The cave-like room was roughly five steps wide and appeared to be empty.

"That looks pretty tunnel-like to me," Billy said.

Jake agreed and continued forward, shining the light above and below alternating with each step to make sure they didn't crack their heads on a low bit of rock or trip over something jutting up from the ground.

The ceiling was no more than a foot above their heads and although uneven looked solid and relatively smooth.

"I guess if this tunnel was going to collapse it would have done it by now," Jake said, thinking out loud.

He kicked a bit of loose dirt or rock across the bumpy floor before shuffling forward, and forward some more, and then some more.

"I wonder if this really goes all the way to the docks?" Jake asked, again letting his thoughts enter his head and fly straight out of his mouth.

The prospect was a daunting one.

He was feeling the damp and cold, and the claustrophobia was beginning to set in the further they got from the entrance—they could barely see the light behind them now. They had come a good fifteen metres; fifty feet, from the hole and the tunnel in front of them showed no sign of ending.

The single beam of light from the phone, and the fading light from the hole were playing tricks on his eyes.

And the harder he tried not to think of ghosts and the gruesome stories he'd been told about the Trow's cellars, the more he thought he was seeing things.

For a few, long minutes they continued forward, Jake continuing his ceiling to floor sweeping routine with the light.

Then something dark caught Jake's eye, causing him to shine the light down and to the right.

"What's that? Do you see it?" Jake asked, straining his eyes to try and decipher if the thing he was looking at was deserving of further investigation.

"Look. Down there."

Jake balanced his phone on a piece of rock on the ground, so the beam was shining on the right side of the tunnel wall near the ground, then knelt down with his arms outstretched moving his hands over the rock in front of him.

"What is it?" Billy asked, staring hard at the back of Jake's head, which was blocking his line of sight to whatever Jake was investigating.

"There's some sort of ledge carved in to the wall. It's like a slot or hole or whatever but… I think there's more. I'm not sure but I think there's something at the back of it."

Jake picked up his phone again and shined it directly at the newly-found gap, which was no more than one metre; around three feet, high, and less than a metre; around three feet, wide.

He thought it looked like a shoe rack carved in to the rock and laughed to himself picturing rows of pirate boots lined up neatly on the ledge.

After shining the light at every angle, it began to look like he'd been mistaken.

"I think that's just the back of the wall," said Billy, taking over for a bit. "Yeh there's nothing. Fuck. I thought we had something for a minute there.

"Wait… to the left. There's a… it looks like a box or something hidden away to the right.

"It is! Man. They went to the effort of digging a concealed ledge within a concealed ledge. Whatever's in that box has got to be important!"

Billy stood up and they looked at each other excitedly in the gloom. "How do we get it out?" asked Jake.

"Good question. It looks pretty lodged in, but I think if we're careful and get down at the right angle, we can reach it by hand. And by we, I mean you—your arms are smaller than mine."

"Great," Jake replied, shuffling down on to his knees, then his stomach so he could get his shoulder low to the ground to give himself the best chance of reaching their prize.

Another minute passed as Jake fished about in the rock-face ledge, his fingers brushing the edge of what felt like a tin box.

"FUCK! I definitely felt it move that time, one hundred percent there's something there, but I can't quite get a grip on it," said Jake in frustration.

"Here. Give me a try."

Jake pulled his arm free and got up on his knees while Billy flattened himself on the ground.

"I had a bit of wriggle room so you should be able to fit," Jake said.

Jake held his breath while he watched his friend concentrate like a locksmith trying to pick a lock.

Finally, Billy said quietly, "I think I've got it, whatever it is. Help keep me steady while I try and bring it out, I don't have a great grip on it, but I think it'll budge."

Slowly they retracted Billy's arm, making sure there were no sudden movements and Billy did all he could to maintain his grasp.

"Gently does it," said Jake quietly.

CHAPTER 3: THE CONTAINER

Billy edged the container closer towards them. The metal box didn't come easy and seemed to be weighed down.

"I don't know if it's just wishful thinking, but it feels heavy," Billy said. Then they both heard it.

An unmistakable clinking sound coming from inside the box as it jarred on a bit of rubble near the edge of the ledge. They could see it now and there was no mistaking it, there was definitely something in it.

Billy continued to pull it free with his right hand and caught it with his left as it dropped off the ledge, again causing whatever was inside to clink loudly.

Jake shone the light on its rusty exterior, and just had time to think that it reminded him of something his nan would keep a Christmas cake in, or some sort of ration box from the war, before another light flashed behind them and they heard a voice.

"Hey, anyone in there?" It was the barman.

They were luckily far enough inside the tunnel now that his light beam fell short of hitting them, and the barman sounded unsure as to whether to pursue or call the police, as if weighing up whether Billy and Jake had left with the others and he just hadn't noticed, or whether they were actually crazy enough to have crawled inside the dark hole in the wall he was now puzzling over.

"Come on, we need to get out of here," Billy whispered, wrapping his arm carefully around the container and urging Jake to press ahead away from the light.

Jake didn't fancy explaining to the barman, or worse the police, what they were doing inside there and hurried ahead in to the gloom dismissing his up down light tactic for a more trot-forward-and-hope-for-the-best tactic.

They continued forward in complete silence for another fifteen minutes, their surroundings barely changing.

"What if this is a dead end?" Jake exclaimed, turning around to check if Billy was still behind him as much as anything else.

Billy's face was a ghoulish mask of concentration in the light of the phone.

"We're nearly there, I'm sure of it. And if we got in at that end as easily as we did then chances are we'll be able to get out just as easily," he said, lying. Billy was thinking exactly the same thing as Jake but had decided there was no point in voicing his concerns or dwelling on them, they were here now.

For another fifteen minutes they trudged forward, going as fast as the tunnel, and the light, would permit them.

Jake did his best to push the stories, and the ghosts, from his mind but it was becoming increasingly more difficult with every step.

"Wait," Jake said, stopping suddenly. "Can you feel that?"

"Yeh, the air has changed. We must be nearly out." Billy's voice broke, in anticipation of fresh air and space.

They scurried forward even faster than before and within a few metres; ten feet, hit a dead-end.

Not immediately seeing a means of escaping, they both began running their hands over every section of the solid surface now confronting them.

"Here!" Jake cried, trying to scratch dirt off the bricks in front of him. "I can see light, it's faint as fuck but I think there's a gap here."

Billy joined in, clawing at any finger-hold he could find to see if he could dislodge a loose brick and force an opening somewhere.

After some success, another idea dawned on him and he took a couple of steps backward.

"Needs more force—like how we got in," he said. "Stand to the side."

Jake pressed himself against the left tunnel wall and turned the light against the section they'd identified as being their most likely means of getting out of there.

Billy lined himself up and aimed a big, right boot at the spot the light was focused on.

He connected dead on where he'd been aiming and while the bricks didn't fly out of the wall like both of them had been praying they would, there was a resounding THUNK as three or four of them moved significantly further backwards.

"Yes! We got this," Billy shouted triumphantly, lining himself up again.

Another kick, another THUNK, and this time one of the bricks almost came completely free. Billy gave it a push with his hand and watched as it dropped out the other side leaving a small, square hole, and letting fresh air rush in to the tunnel.

They worked feverishly taking turns to line up and kick the vulnerable spot, then pushing and clawing with their fingers to finish off whatever they'd manage to loosen up.

Within fifteen minutes they were through, and on some sort of river bank looking up at the stars and breathing heavily.

"Oh, fuck, I'm never, ever going in another fucking tunnel again," Jake declared, looking around at their new surroundings. "Wait... I know here. That's the Arnolfini on the other side of the water—we're on the harbourside! The tunnel must have taken us right underneath the harbour."

"Makes sense," Billy said, delighted they knew their location. "A pirate tunnel that comes out where pirates probably kept their ships."

"Yeh, look at those big houses up there." Jake pointed up the slope they were on, and in the opposite direction to the arts centre he'd spotted and used to ground his location.

"I bet they used to bring their ships in here then take their cargo up there for storage, or to sell or whatever. We need to head up that way then we can get back around and home!" Just as Jake began to start climbing up Billy stopped him.

"Want to take a quick peek before we go? I reckon we've got time, even if the barman called the police it'll take them a while to arrive, and even longer to get through that tunnel—plus, we'd see their lights coming a mile from here."

Jake nodded and Billy carefully put the tin container down on a somewhat even patch of ground.

Illuminated by the moonlight, they could make out the container was dark grey all over. If there had been any markings on the exterior of the box then they'd either worn away or they were covered in such thick dust that they were now completely invisible.

"After you man," Billy whispered, gesturing to his friend to open the tin.

Jake carefully found the edges of the lid and tried to ease them off, but it was jammed on tight.

"You hold it down around the base and I'll try and get the lid off. There's no way anyone's opened this in years."

It took a few minutes of careful manoeuvring and force before the lid scraped off an inch on one side.

"Got it!"

They glanced at each other for a split-second and grinned before Jake did the honours and revealed its contents.

"Whoa. We've definitely found some sort of stash all right," whispered Billy, transfixed.

"Bottles…" Jake paused, counting in his head. "Three of them." He lifted one out.

It was medium-sized, with a fat body and stocky neck. A square label with an uneven circle drawn on it was stuck to the front, with various patterns drawn inside the circle in faded black ink.

"Probably around seventy centilitres; almost three cups, and I'd bet on rum," said Jake to himself.

He put the bottle back in its row. They were in remarkable condition if they were as old as he thought they were.

"Why would a pirate go to the trouble of stashing three bottles in a hidden compartment in a hidden passageway?" asked Billy.

"Fits actually. I guess they used this passage to cart illegal booze from the pub to the docks, and they kept it hidden here while it was in transit. Maybe they kept a load down there and then sent some signal for their people to come up through the tunnel and collect it, loaded it on ships, and carted it off somewhere to make a fortune?"

"Yeh, but, three of them? Doesn't make sense," stated Billy, frowning.

"I know," Jake agreed. "But whatever they are, they're a find. I mean they must have been down there for the best part of three hundred years, if they really were put there by pirates. Let's get out of the cold and damp and take them to the flat so we can get a better look."

CHAPTER 4: THE MAP

Jake sat down at his cramped kitchen table, placing the bottles in front of him.

"This is all a bit surreal, isn't it?" he said half to Billy, who was making a coffee and a tea for Jake, and half to himself.

"Yeh, it's like something from a film. Turns out every American's idea that the UK is one big history book is totally true."

He joined Jake at the table, put the cups down, and picked up one of the three bottles, holding it up to the light.

The storm clouds had left long enough for a bit of sunshine to break through. It was shining on the golden orange liquid through the window, making the whole bottle glow, and the label almost translucent.

Almost.

The map was unmistakable.

This was a different bottle to the one Jake had looked at outside the tunnel, but it also had a jagged shape sketched out on the label.

In the light and with fresh eyes, it was now easy to see the uneven shape was in fact an island, and the scrawls inside the jagged boundary were indications of the terrain, peaks, presumably meant mountains, steep hills or high ground, and trees must mean jungles and forests, waves for water, and curves at the edge of the map looked like beaches.

Each bottle had a different island drawn on it with different markings inside.

There were also markings neither Billy nor Jake understood, but spent many hours, cups of tea and coffee, and cigarettes daydreaming over.

"Let's go back to the thing that kind of looks like the infinity symbol on this bottle but isn't. I've Googled everything I can think of and nothing's coming up. What the hell is it?" said Jake. His enthusiasm for the subject only gaining in intensity despite the hours of fruitless research that had already been done.

Precisely drawn on the edge of one of the tree symbols was a diagonal oval with another diagonal oval crossing it in the opposite direction.

"It looks like an X marks the spot, but why they didn't just draw it with straight lines beats me. I still don't get this anchor symbol," Billy said, pointing to a straight line with the bottom half of a circle attached. "It's right next to this mountain or hill or whatever, but that makes no sense. If it was on the water I'd get it... unless there's some hidden water under there that connects to the sea somewhere. Let's make a list of all the markings and note down what each could be."

Jake nodded. "And let's keep a list of all the islands and try and narrow it down some more. It's likely that these three islands are close together so that should help us a bit."

The Caribbean had seemed the obvious place to start and they'd been pouring over Google maps, comparing craggy coastlines with the ink drawings, noting down any islands that looked similar.

One island was an off circle with many jagged points and cuts around its edges, another looked kind of like a nose with beaches all along the south and west and rocks and trees on the east and north, and one looked exactly like a bird's claw.

The arch of the claw looked like a large cove, with a lot of jungle or forest on the top of the foot and higher ground or mountains going up the ankle and the start of the leg.

As well as studying the Caribbean islands, they'd also expanded the search to include central and north America in case the islands on the map were somewhere around there, as well as parts of the Mediterranean and Africa.

It threw up quite a few possibilities, but two of the islands they kept coming back to had almost identical landmarks to the bottle map equivalents and Jake and Billy were convinced they'd found two out of the three destinations.

"This one has to be Barbados," Billy said, raising one bottle in the air for probably the fifth time. "Rocks and trees on one side, and nothing but beaches on the other. It has to be."

"And this one's Antigua," said Jake, holding up another. "There are so many inlets, cuts, coves, and sharp edges on this map that match up with Antigua, it has to be there."

"So, where's this bird's claw then?" Billy asked, holding up the third.

They'd had no luck tracking down the third at all, despite it being by far the most distinctive in shape.

"No idea," said Jake. "But two out of three ain't bad, and we're pretty certain we've got those right. Chances are the other island's near the other two, at least in the Caribbean, maybe it's absolutely tiny and not on Google maps."

"Could be," agreed Billy. "And even if it isn't close, hopefully we can track down these markings in Antigua and Barbados and we'll find some clues that'll help us track it down. No doubt if there's something of real value to be found it'll be on the one that's harder to find. Seems like a very pirate thing to do to me, a map within a map sort of thing."

"Yep, agreed. I think we've found about all we can from here."

Feeling pretty pleased with their earlier cover-up job of the hole they'd made, and the progress they'd made with the maps, they felt relaxed enough to break for a sleep, followed by a late lunch and a couple of beers.

"When does anyone, ever, get the chance to live out a proper adventure like this?" Billy asked. "It's like someone picked us for this chance and practically punched us in the face with it to make sure we don't miss it."

"I know, right?" Jake was just as up for it now.

Rested, confident their secret discovery was still theirs to uncover in their own time, and a few drinks down, both boys were wild-eyed and ready to get on a plane.

"So, we're really doing this, huh? I mean, we're just going to book a couple of tickets to Antigua and Barbados, maybe hire a Jeep or something, load a bunch of supplies in the back, and go hunt some long-lost treasure?"

"Sounds kinda crazy when you say it out loud. No idea where I'm going to get the money from," Jake said, fearing the bubble was about to inexplicably burst. I have some savings but flights, hotels, and car hire in the Caribbean is going to cost a fortune."

"Seriously, man, don't worry about the money. I've got a savings account full of guilt cash. My mom pays off her conscience by adding thousands of dollars to my account, so she never has to actually see me, and my dad deposits obscene chunks of money to justify the amount of time he spends at work, and all the childhood memories he missed out on. I'm not trying to be flash, but we can live it up and it won't make a dent, and I can't think of a single thing that would be money better spent. Can you?"

Billy's parents had split when he was younger. They'd both worked at the same bank and had cash. Billy had stayed with his dad and his mum had made little effort to see him since.

She did, however, always make sure his account was full, as did his dad. He was their only child and even if they weren't so great at the making him feel loved part, they definitely made up for it in the being taken care of department.

Jake hated the thought of someone else paying for anything. He liked being independent and resourceful. But Billy made a compelling case and the offer was too tempting.

"I can't disagree with you on that one. Aside from actually buying an island, this is pretty much as good as it gets. But I'll pay my way as much as I can. Let's have a look at the costs and see what the damage is going to be."

CHAPTER 5: FLIGHT

Jake sat back in his seat and examined his surroundings.

He'd been on a few flights around Europe, but only one long-haul flight in his life, and that had been to New York last year to visit Billy.

He was in row eight at the front of the plane in the aisle seat. Billy was to his left in the middle and the window seat was empty.

He looked past Billy out at the runway where he could see people scurrying around making the final preparations before take-off. The rain had infiltrated London as well as Bristol, and the workers were grimacing from the onslaught of water swirling around the tarmac and slapping them in the face from all angles.

Jake could almost feel their discomfort and looked away, turning his attention back inside the cabin.

The crew were going through the motion of informing the passengers that, should anything happen, the best thing to do would be to keep completely calm and curl up in a ball, or as close as you could, while staying in the seat of the plane.

Because that'll help, he thought sarcastically to himself. He took his phone out of his pocket and opened the Caribbean guide book he'd downloaded, skipping straight to the section on Barbados, their first destination.

The intro was all about incredible beaches with fine, white sand, and turquoise waters. He'd never been anywhere this tropical or exotic in his life and had to take a moment to fully appreciate that this was really happening.

"Still hasn't sunk in for me either," said Billy, reading his friend's expression.

"I went to Hawaii a couple of times when I was a kid. My parents have a house there, but I can't remember a lot. Mainly arguing, and I certainly didn't get to explore. I'm psyched that we're going island-hopping in the Caribbean. I mean that's a trip of a lifetime stuff as it is, and then when I think about what we're actually doing when we get there… man, this is awesome!"

Jake looked back outside into the rain and grey, so grey. "Yep, it really is."

The plane grumbled to life, the cabin crew strapped themselves in, and with a noise that sounded to Jake like an electronic robot moving its arms up and down a few times, they headed down the runway.

As soon as they were in the sky, and the seatbelt sign had gone out, Billy was pressing the button for assistance.

"Can I help you, sir?" One of the attendants appeared over Jake's shoulder, looking at Billy.

"Yes, please. Could we get a couple of whiskey and cokes?"

"We'll be coming around shortly with the drink trolley…"

"Okay, great, thank you. We've never flown before." He lied. "We're just a bit excited." Billy grinned.

The attendant paused and smiled back. "I can grab a couple now quickly and we can see if you're ready for a top up when we reach you with the trolley."

The woman turned and walked off, returning swiftly with the drinks, plastic glasses, and ice.

"Thanks so much," said Billy, smiling.

"Enjoy," replied the woman, smiling, before walking away.

These sorts of exchanges hadn't been uncommon during the time Jake had known Billy.

He was a good-looking guy, but not exceptionally so. He had wavy, dark brown, almost black hair which was cut fairly short and pushed up above his forehead to one side, and he had dark brown stubble that was verging on a beard.

He was normally clean cut and pristine in his appearance for work but preferred to look a little less Ivy League on his own time.

But his persuasive power came from his demeanour not his looks. Despite being only in his mid-twenties, Billy had a gravitas to his character, and a genuineness that shined through immediately and either got people on side or got their backs up.

Normally, if the person was of the opposite sex, it was the former.

Billy poured the drinks for himself and his friend, handed one to Jake, and raised his glass. "Cheers."

"Cheers, that's a good skill, the whole getting people to do stuff for you without even asking, when it's highly unlikely they'd do the same thing for anyone else." Jake laughed.

"It may come in handy when we're there. Especially if we need to go off the beaten track and need some guides, which I'm guessing we will."

"I agree with you on that. I can't imagine there's going to be an excursion to any of the points on these maps, not like we can just ask at our hotel reception."

They took deep sips from their drinks and relaxed back in their seats.

CHAPTER 6: AMY

Amy had hung on every word.

She'd been on the lookout for anyone remotely attractive from the moment they sat down and the two lads who'd walked past, and were now sitting in the row behind, had not escaped her attention.

She'd found them intriguing, even before they started talking about their mysterious trip.

Amy hadn't gathered many details, but she'd heard enough to know there was more than sun and sea on their itinerary, and she desperately wanted to know what it was.

Anything to distract herself from her current situation. "Nut," offered Issy, looking at her friend with curiosity.

"Relax will you? That's what we're here for. You look like you're trying to crawl out of your own skin," Issy said.

"I'm fine, just a bit fidgety. As soon as we take off and I get a drink in my hand, I'll be great."

Amy paused, then mouthed silently, "Have you seen?" Making subtle-ish pointing gestures to the two seats directly behind them.

Issy rolled her eyes. "Mmhm. But since we haven't even taken off, yet, I haven't paid too much attention."

"They're up to something," Amy continued to mouth. "And they're hot."

Issy laughed, mouthing back, "What do you mean?"

Amy shrugged and tried not to turn around. "I'll tell you later," she replied, back to normal volume.

Turning away from her friend and towards the aisle to see if she could trouble a flight attendant for a drink, she felt the back of her seat move backward as someone pulled on it to lever themselves out of their own seat.

Billy let go of Amy's seat in front of him, climbed in to the aisle, turned away from Amy, and reached up to open the bin above his head and retrieve his headphones from his bag.

Amy didn't hesitate, reached over and pinched his ass.

"Ahh, fuck!" Billy grunted. He half jumped forward and half spun round at the same time, lost his balance, and almost sat on a serious-looking middle-aged man's lap.

"S-sorry, I ... sorry," he said, edging away.

He looked at Amy. She was grinning broadly. "For fuck's sake."

Issy put her head in her hands. "Smooth."

Amy laughed.

Billy's mouth dropped open to say something, but no words came out. He was still trying to figure out what the hell was going on.

"Sorry, I thought it'd be a good ice-breaker," she said. "Yeh, I mean.. yeh… I didn't really think that through."

"Can you take your seat, sir, we're about to take off," the flight attendant interjected.

"Of course." Glad to be saved from this awkward encounter, Billy gratefully sat back in his seat and buckled himself up again.

"What was that all about?" asked Jake, having only caught the end.

"Man, I have no idea. The girl in the seat in front just pinched my ass. And she's hot!" he mouthed.

Jake looked through the gap in the seats.

He was sitting one to the left of Billy, and Amy was in front and to the right of him.

He could see her two bare legs popping out from beneath a white skirt, crossed, with the top leg bouncing up and down like she was unable to sit still.

Occasionally, she leaned over to talk to her friend and he caught a look at her brown hair, cut to the same length as her face and flicking up towards her lips.

"Damn. She *is* hot," he whispered to Billy.

"I told you, dude, but I have no idea what just happened."

Jake looked at his friend in disbelief, a bit jealous, and a little bit in awe.

It made him sit back and daydream about what could happen next. If this was happening before they'd even left the runway, he couldn't wait to see how the rest of the trip unfolded.

He was completely out of his comfort zone and couldn't have been happier.

CHAPTER 7: ISSY

"Great move by the way. Now he thinks you're a complete psycho," Issy hissed.

"He does not, he's totally hard for me. But, yeh, that was probably a weird way to go." Amy looked at her friend and they both grinned.

This trip was meant to be a distraction from crap boyfriends.

Well, one crap boyfriend—Amy's—who'd decided to fuck some girl from his work one night Amy was out with her friends.

Except she wasn't.

Amy's friends had cancelled, and she'd come home to find her boyfriend of three years kneeling in front of a girl. Both naked. His head had been obscuring her lower body and her ass had been pressed against the bookshelf Amy's parents had insisted on getting them from Ikea the last time they'd been over to visit from Australia.

Worst of all, Amy had made eye-contact with the girl, who had been torn between pleasure and terror, and Amy couldn't get the image out of her head. The exchange that followed was brutal. And now, Amy lived alone.

Hence the need for a spontaneous trip to Barbados with her best friend Issy, who was a little worried her closest ally had lost her mind following the incident.

Amy continued to jiggle one leg on top of the other. She wanted to look around but even she wasn't that brave. "What are they doing?" she asked out of the side of her mouth.

Issy took a peek between the two seats and quickly glanced back. She met Jake's eyes square on. She froze, then retreated.

"Um, well, the guy that you didn't assault is staring at us!" she whispered.

"Is he hot too?"

"What the fuck is wrong with you?" An awkward silence.

"Yeh, he's fucking hot! Now we have eight hours to make small talk," Issy mumbled shortly after.

"Don't worry, I got this." Amy jumped up from her seat, reached up and opened the overhead compartment in front of her and rummaged around for effect.

She turned to find Billy staring at her thighs, and said, "I'm going to need to swap seats with your friend—that work for you?"

Billy smiled at her.

"Are you kidding me??" Jake jumped in. "Excuse me, but the seatbelt sign is still on…" The plane had only just taken off.

"Okay, cool, as soon as we're at altitude or whatever I'll come and sit back there and you can come sit next to Issy, okay." She hadn't asked, she'd told.

Billy and Jake sat in their seats staring at the seatbelt sign. "We're not really going to swap seats, are we?"

"Man have you seen that girl's legs?"

Jake paused, he had. "Yeh, that's fine for you, but what about…"

"Hey! I'm not exactly thrilled about this either!" Issy mumbled between the seats.

Another long, awkward pause followed.

Everyone sat back in their seats and stared at the seatbelt light overhead. *Ding.*

"Awesome." Amy jumped up from her seat.

"Come on, pretty boy, get up and go sit next to Issy," she said, looking at Jake.

Jake looked properly at Amy for the first time.

She was around one hundred sixty-seven centimetres; five foot six, with brown hair that came to her chin and flicked up at the ends, big brown eyes, pink lips, and a petite body beneath a short, white skirt, and blue top.

"Stop staring and move."

He was a little annoyed. This was distracting them from finding—well, who knew what—but mostly he was just hoping Amy's friend was as hot as she was and that maybe, just maybe, she'd be even more forward than her friend during this flight.

As he brushed past Amy she said, "You'll need to lead." And he could barely believe his ears.

Jake dropped down in to Amy's still warm seat, took a moment, then looked over to his left.

Issy was nothing like her friend.

Although she was sitting down, she was clearly taller, and more athletically built.

"Hi. I'm Isabella… Issy." She offered Jake her hand.

Issy was a lot calmer than her friend and seemed mildly interested in the whole scenario more than anything else.

He shook her hand and smiled, bashfully.

She turned away and picked up the newspaper from the seat in front of her, turned straight to the football at the back, and began to read.

"What was the score?" Jake asked. "I totally forgot England was playing."

Issy looked up at Jake.

She paused, as if deciding which way to go. How she answered now would either open the door to eight hours of chat with this boy or she could slam it closed and enjoy eight hours of movies and music. She'd fully stocked her phone with new albums before they left.

"They won, 1-0. Really good goal apparently, side-foot volley from the edge of the area," she replied.

"Nice. You play?" Jake asked, unable to help himself looking at her athletic physique as he posed the question.

"Mostly I sit on the bench at the moment. Still trying to get in to the first team. I'm in the reserves for one of the London clubs, I'm a winger," she said, unsure of how much to give away.

"How about you?"

"That's awesome. I've never played anywhere near that level. Actually, I've never been that great at football. I'm just not that great with a ball. I surf a bit," he added, realising he kind of wanted to impress this girl.

"Nice! Maybe you can teach me when we get to Barbados."

Issy turned back to her paper and Jake looked away.

He tried to think about the plans he'd discussed with Billy, about how they were going to hire some scuba stuff and a little boat and explore the coast, and hopefully find the first marking they'd identified on the map, but this blonde footballer was clouding things.

And God knows what was going on behind him.

CHAPTER 8: GETTING TO KNOW YOU

"So, you're Australian, huh?" Billy ventured, having recovered his voice and some of his swagger.

"Born and raised in Sydney, moved to England when I was eighteen, met the love of my life and planned to marry him, turned out he was a complete cunt. What else?" She smiled.

Billy couldn't find any level ground.

It felt like he was in some sort of earthquake and every time he thought he'd found a safe spot to catch his breath, the earth crumbled away beneath his feet.

He wasn't used to this.

"Marriage is a waste of time," he said, trying to gain the upper hand.

"How so?"

"Actually, I have no idea why I said that." He shrugged, embarrassed.

"It wasn't all bad, and to be honest it's cliché but I'm glad I found out he was a cunt now and not, you know, after we'd bought a house and had two girls and a boy. Not that I was planning or anything." She laughed.

"True." Another piece of dirt disappeared, and Billy lost his footing again.

They paused, only Billy felt uncomfortable. Amy ran her hand through her hair and then stretched.

"So, where you staying?" she asked, eventually.

"Needham's Point. It's on the south coast."

"Island Spa Apartments, right?"

"Uh… yeh." Billy was stunned.

"We saw the offer online too, looks nice, especially the infinity pool." Another pause.

"That's ridiculous! I mean, it's not that small an island."

"True, but it's a new place and they obviously want to make sure it's full in its first season."

"Did you get two separate apartments or are you sharing with pretty boy?" She looked ahead in Jake's direction.

"Two apartments. Pretty boy? I mean, we thought we'd go for it right. Trip of a lifetime and all that."

"Where's that drink?" Amy said, distracted. "You need a top up? You're out."

"Whiskey and coke."

Amy pressed a button above her head.

"So, you have two apartments too? You could be next door, this is crazy!"

"No, we're sharing a room. Not as flash as you… name?"

"Billy. And?"

"Amy, and that's Issy pretty boy is hitting on."

Billy had never come across anyone so forward in his life.

He sensed partly it was her situation and underneath the bravado she was hurting, but mostly she just seemed—fierce, or fearless, or both.

"We'll have two rum and cokes. And can you get the same for our two friends in front, please and thank you."

She turned to Billy. "So, what's your story? American in the UK heading to a tropical island… actually forget that. I don't care. Tell me you're single then tell me where you're taking me when we get there."

Billy laughed, a proper 'the ground has stopped fucking about' laugh and relaxed in his seat.

"Well, I guess we're stuck with you now. I've heard there's some pretty good beach bars and seafood places near where we're staying. Sound good?"

"That'll do." She smiled, got up, pulled her skirt straight and disappeared towards the bathroom.

CHAPTER 9: ARRIVAL

As the plane tipped first one side then the other as it circled Grantley Adams International Airport, Jake gathered his magazines, headphones, and thoughts together.

The flight had been far more eventful than he could have imagined, and given they'd found a long-lost treasure map—three long-lost treasure maps—and that's why they were on the plane in the first place, was some pretty good going to his mind. It hadn't been bad eventful either.

At first, when Amy had entered their world he'd been apprehensive. She'd been so forward, and well, intrusive, that he thought she might ruin the flight and get in the way of their planning.

Then when he'd discovered they were staying at the same place as them, his heart had sunk.

Finding out two attractive women wanted to talk to them and were staying in the same holiday resort should have filled him with excitement, and ordinarily a little dread too at the prospect he'd have to make small-talk.

He'd never had great chat, and that initial getting-to-know-you stage he'd always found pretty nerve-racking. But he'd made such a big discovery with his best friend, he didn't want their adventure to be derailed.

He'd suddenly felt very protective over their secret.

Who knew how much the bottles that were wrapped in clothes in Billy's bag in the hold were worth on their own, let alone if the maps on them actually led to some sort of ancient treasure.

This was their opportunity to set themselves up for the rest of their lives. Well, Billy already had that, this was his chance.

More than that, they could say they'd made their money as explorers and adventurers. It definitely had more of a ring to it than saying, 'Oh, me? I work in accounts as an assistant to the regional manager,' or 'I work in legal administration.'

This was a chance to make history.

Sure, it could all amount to nothing. And his daydreams of extreme optimism filled with grand discoveries, shiny, gold objects, and artifacts steeped in forgotten history were regularly disrupted by bouts of doubt, where he was convinced the bottles they'd found were worthless, and the maps nothing more than a dead, drunk sailor's scrawls.

But he didn't really believe the doubts. Even during his most sceptical moods, he was certain the bottles alone were worth something.

And he didn't want anyone to take this, whatever this panned out to be, away from them.

But as the plane's wheels hit then bounced along the runway before more smoothly rolling along the tarmac and bringing the plane to a halt, he felt he had been worrying about nothing.

He'd spent most of the flight in Amy's seat next to Issy. She'd been easy to talk to, they'd laughed a lot but also given each other a break whenever things felt a bit too intense or forced.

Jake watched a couple of films and Issy listened to a lot of music. She said music was huge for her and she always listened to different types of music ahead of training, a match, or to unwind afterwards; win, lose, or draw.

He definitely found her attractive, but guessed she got plenty of attention.

She wasn't wearing a lot of make-up, just a bit around her eyes and her eye-lashes had mascara or were fake, and she had on fitted, grey, three-quarter-length jogging bottoms, bright white running shoes, and white top.

He wasn't sure if there'd been anything between them. A couple of times it felt like they were flirting but the conversation always landed back on more plutonic ground and Jake didn't push for anything and neither did Issy.

Behind them things calmed down once the flight was properly underway too. Amy seemed to relax and was much calmer. Her fierceness retreating for the moment, and the conversation flowed easily between her and Billy.

A common ground for them was comparing Sydney to New York and using any major differences to savagely make fun of the other's country of birth.

Best of all was when they stumbled across something that Australia and America did so much better than Britain, turning their mirth and attention to the two Brits in front of them, who were sometimes aware, sometimes not.

They'd also had a few drinks, which no doubt had aided the constant conversation.

"So, you two just fancied a romantic getaway then, huh?" Amy had teased at one point.

"Yeh, that's exactly it." Billy laughed.

"Actually... we came out here because we are looking for something," he added, lowering his voice.

* * *

Billy had known as soon as the words had spilled from his mouth that he'd made a mistake. But now they were coming to land, the booze having completely worn off, his mind turned to what may lay ahead for them—and he regretted telling Amy more than ever.

He hadn't told Amy everything.

He'd been tipsy and just wanted to impress her, and to get the impression out of her head that he'd taken his best mate for a spa-break in the Caribbean.

He'd said that Jake had been left some stuff from a relative that had recently passed away. And said family member had connections to the Caribbean, and in his safe there'd been an ancient case of rum with three bottles in it. Each one with a map on its label, one of which looked like a map of Barbados showing a few landmarks.

That's all.

Fuck, fuck, fuck. I practically told her everything, Billy thought to himself, screwing his eyes up.

The only things he'd left out or changed were where they'd gotten the bottles, or what they actually suspected was on them.

He'd made it sound more like this was some adventurous way of tracing back Jake's family tree, going back to his roots and all that.

He cringed as he remembered giving it the big sell.

Painting the picture that he was the sympathetic friend supporting his best mate after he'd lost a close family member. Had he said grandad or uncle? He couldn't remember. He'd also told her they were both the type to say 'fuck it' drop everything and go on some crazy adventure at the drop of a hat.

The second part was true at least.

Jake's going to kill me. Hopefully she was more drunk than I was, he thought to himself as they filed off the plane and the heat hit them.

The air smelt tropical.

It was just after three in the afternoon, and it must have been around thirty-five degrees and humid too.

Pitch-black clouds parked at the edge of the skyline, as if waiting for a signal to march across the sky and cause chaos.

"This is awesome," Jake exclaimed right behind him.

Billy grinned. "Yeh, man, this is pretty damn cool." His shame was passing, perhaps they wouldn't see a lot more of these girls and the bottles would never come up.

Yeh, it's totally fine, he thought to himself. All good.

CHAPTER 10: SUSPICION

Amy watched Jake and his friend walk ahead in front of them in to the airport.

They were talking intently, as if they didn't want anyone else to hear their conversation.

Amy grabbed Issy's arm. "What do you think they're up to?"

"Well, looks kind of like they're excited to be in Barbados, and I can't disagree with them there. And they're probably talking about us, I imagine," Issy replied.

"Actually, I don't think they are." Amy didn't take her eyes off them. "When you guys were watching a movie we carried on drinking and Billy got very chatty. He told me they were here because Jake had been left three ancient bottles of rum by an uncle who'd just died. Apparently, they're legit and date back to 1650 or 1700 or something, and each bottle has a map on it, with different points marked on each of them. Billy told me that bit as if he was daydreaming out loud and when he saw how into it I was, he kind of freaked out. He then told me they had decided to come here because they wanted to check out the maps, and what's marked on them, to see where his family came from. But I'm sure that last bit is BS."

"You've lost me," Issy stated.

"I've gone over the conversation in my head a hundred times since—and I'm convinced he was telling the truth. About the maps, at least. I'm not at all buying the other stuff."

"So, they've got some maps. I still don't get it?" Issy looked bored.

"I heard them talking when we first got on too. They were so secretive and excited. I don't know how they got hold of those maps but one hundred percent they exist, and that's why they're here. I just don't think they're tracing back any family tree, I think they're hunting for treasure. And sounds like they have a pretty good lead."

Issy laughed loudly. "Ha. That's classic. So, we just happened to take a flight with two twenty-something adventurers who are about to strike gold?"

Amy smiled but was deadly serious. "Pretty much, yeh! Surely, you're excited by this too?"

"I want in, whatever it is they're looking for. I want to be there when they find it."

"If you find stuff then legally you get a share or a reward or I don't know something. Imagine if they do strike gold!" Amy added.

Issy was thinking about it now. "And you're sure these maps weren't left to them by their dying uncle?"

"Not one hundred percent sure, no, but even if they were, I still want in.

"I think there's something shady going on. I think somehow they've managed to get their hands on someone else's winning lottery ticket and they're here to cash it in and run off with the money before anyone finds out."

CHAPTER 11: THE APARTMENTS

Jake looked out of the mini-bus window wide-eyed.

"This is a bit different to what we left behind, hey?" he half said to Jake and half to himself.

The windows were open, and the air-con was on, but the heat was everywhere and unstoppable.

Jake had swapped his jeans for some shorts at the airport before they set off, which he was grateful for, but could still feel the sweat prickle his skin and occasionally drip down his back. He felt like he was in a sauna.

Everything was as bright as it was hot. The streets were dusty and dry, but their surroundings were unmistakably Caribbean. Many of the houses were pastel yellows, reds, blues, and greens, and there was plenty of plant life.

Tiny speakers inside their mini-bus were blaring out reggae music. Jake wasn't sure if it was for their benefit, but he liked it.

He couldn't get over how vibrant the place was, even from the tiny amount he'd seen so far. The entire island had a population of under three hundred thousand—much smaller than Bristol—but, to him, it felt like it was buzzing with activity everywhere he looked.

The new resort they were staying at was just back from Pebble Beach. It had only been open a few weeks and they'd done a big promotion to make sure it got off to a good start.

Jake recognized quite a few other faces besides Amy and Issy on their mini-bus from the plane and guessed they were all heading to the same destination.

"I think we're here," Jake heard Issy say from the front of the bus. He saw the pastel yellow sign with turquoise writing Island Spa.

One by one they piled off the mini-bus and were surprised, and happy, to find it was even hotter outside.

None of them cared they were wearing too many clothes in too much heat, this was the best bit—the beginning of the holiday. The weather was exceeding all expectations and each of them knew within minutes they'd be able to jump in to a crystal-clear swimming pool or the turquoise sea, followed most likely by some type of cocktail.

Jake, Billy, Amy, and Issy gathered their suitcases in a pile by the minibus. Jake noticed that they'd instinctively fallen into a foursome, but he seemed to be the only one who was conscious of this or had any objection.

Once they'd unloaded everything, Jake and Billy put their backpacks on their shoulders and motioned for the two girls to lead the way.

Both Issy and Amy had big hard-shell suitcases that wheeled along just fine, until there was a kerb or bump.

Amy struggled with one particularly big step up to the front door and Billy grabbed her suitcase and gave her a hand.

"Thanks." She smiled.

The reception was stunning. Everything was white, light, and airy with bright splashes of colour to give it that island feel.

They took a seat along one big sofa with bright yellow and red cushions while they waited for other guests in front of them to get checked in.

It was a bit of a squash, with Billy and Amy pressed up against each other in the middle.

The resort staff offered them a glass of rum punch while they waited to check in. Once they all had their keys, they headed off together to find their accommodations.

Issy and Amy came across their room first, and Billy and Jake went in to see how it looked.

"Wow," Issy said. "This is incredible."

It was really modern with everything hooked up to some sort of technology to turn on the lights, TV, or jacuzzi by voice control, but the decoration was classy without being pretentious.

There were photos of brightly-coloured Caribbean scenes framed in big red and yellow wooden frames.

Both beds were double, with pastel yellow and turquoise covers. The bathroom was beautiful.

"Okay, that's the last time either of you are coming in here." Amy winked. "Let's go find your apartments."

Amy and Issy dropped their bags and they all headed back out in the tropical heat, walking along a small white stone path.

The boys were only a couple of minutes' walk away, past the two swimming pools, one which was attached to a bar you could swim straight up to, and one that had been designed with a perfect view of the coast behind it, so it looked like you were going to swim straight into the sea.

Jake and Billy's apartments were next door to each other and as close to the beach as you could get in this resort.

"Someone splashed the cash," Amy teased.

They went in to the first apartment and had a look around.

"Damn boys! This makes our room look like a hostel," Issy said, heading straight to the huge French doors looking on to the white sand.

The window frames and door panels were all pastel yellow matching the bedding, and there were dashes of bright red and turquoise the same as in the girls' room.

But this one was much bigger, and the view made it.

"It's stunning," Amy said, pushing open the French doors that led to a private terrace.

"All yours, Jake, I'm sure the other one is much the same. Pretty sweet place."

"It's unreal. Cheers, man." Jake put his bag by the bed as he took it all in.

After a nose around the bathroom, which had a giant walk-in shower, they headed outside.

The sky hadn't changed much from when they'd arrived. It was mostly clear and bright blue with plenty of hot sunshine spraying down.

The beach was pristine white sand and just a minute walk from where they were. The clear turquoise-blue sea shimmered invitingly just beyond that. There was a small pier to their right, painted in pastel turquoise, and palm trees sprung out all around them the closer inland you got.

"This place is something else, I mean the beach and your apartment! You might not be coming to our place, but we are definitely hanging out here, after we've kicked you out, of course," Amy said.

"Come on, let's go see how the other one looks and then we have to get in the water."

Jake wanted to go over the maps again now that they were actually here, but Amy's plan was hard to argue with and it was impossible not to want to get in that water, it barely even looked real.

"I'm not coming home," he joked to Billy as they headed over to the last apartment.

CHAPTER 12: HORSES AT DAWN

Jake woke up around five in the morning.

Largely because back home it was around ten in the morning, so his body couldn't stay asleep. But also because his brain couldn't help buzzing about the bottles and being on the island.

He smiled to himself. For the first time in years he finally realised, and accepted, that he'd been drifting.

He'd known it deep down, and he'd even had some people tell him to his face. Billy had brought it up once when he was over in America, and his mum very unsubtly kept repeating he could do anything he wanted to if he just put his mind to it.

The implication was clear, and she was right. He hadn't properly put his mind to anything, for ages.

He'd been asleep, and now he was getting a taste of just how much was on offer, he felt like he never wanted to go back to sleep ever again.

He stepped out on to the terrace expecting there to be a chill. There was a breeze, but it was like warm breath more than anything else. Barely detectable and like everything else here, alive.

He went back inside, pulled on the same ripped, peach-coloured shorts he'd been wearing yesterday, and made himself a coffee.

The apartment blew his mind. He'd never even seen anywhere this nice let alone stayed there.

A cafetière with a selection of fresh ground coffee was provided and it wasn't listed on the room service menu, so he assumed it was complimentary.

Billy had insisted on paying for everything up front and said Jake could pay him back whenever.

Jake had promised to pay back every penny, but he hated to think how much this place cost.

He took his coffee, and the cafetière, in case he fancied a top up, and sat down on a lounge chair out on the terrace, happily preparing to go through his thoughts.

The sky was different shades of pink, dark to light, and the sand now looked a similar colour to his shorts. The sea still seemed to be calling him and he wondered if there was much surf on the island, there were a few waves but nothing too big at the moment.

He went over their day together yesterday.

Billy's apartment had been almost identical to Jake's, the only real difference was the pictures that had been framed on the wall were more coastal of coves, a ship, and beaches. He assumed one or all of the pictures were from Bridgetown, which was a short walk from where they were staying.

The four of them had agreed to do some sight-seeing together, and maybe even hire a car.

He was worried about that. They didn't have all the time in the world, even though, right now, it felt like they did, and Jake wanted to get on the trail as soon as possible.

He knew Billy did too, but maybe a bit less than him.

And he also couldn't deny he was enjoying hanging out with these two girls as much as his friend was. When they'd gone to the sea together yesterday, seeing them in bikinis, it had been extremely hard to keep his eyes on the scenery.

Issy was built like an athlete. She had very little body fat, was lean with muscular, toned legs, obviously from all the football and running, and she had ridiculous abs without looking like a body-builder.

She was a bit taller than Amy, probably around one hundred seventy-seven centimetres; five foot ten, and Jake was one hundred eighty centimetres; five foot eleven. She'd worn a pair of denim shorts and a yellow bikini that had been hard not to stare at.

When she went in the sea she just seemed to cut through the waves effortlessly. Jake had charged in after her and after ten minutes treading water he'd suggested a race, his competitive streak which had been dormant for so long, coming to the fore.

Jake had always been a good swimmer, and he loved water. Swimming, surfing, sailing, and just being near it.

They were out far enough so they couldn't stand up.

"To the pier and back to here, where Billy and Amy are on the beach," Issy had said.

"Three, two, one. Go!"

It had been a good race. They were both strong swimmers but Issy had edged him in the end, and he now wondered whether she'd let him get as close as he had.

He smiled to himself, he'd been going all out.

He'd lost, but it still felt amazing to have really tried.

Amy and Billy had come in and paddled with them a few times but pretty much remained on the beach, sharing the odd cigarette, and chatting.

Billy wasn't as toned as Jake, but he was bigger all round. Billy was one hundred eighty-eight centimetres; six foot two, broad-shouldered, and naturally big-boned.

He had big dark 1980s-style sunglasses on, dark-red swimming shorts with a black palm tree print on them, making him an eye-catching character, even from a distance.

Amy, to no one's surprise, hadn't been shy about getting into her swimwear.

She'd had on a black, high-leg bikini, and sauntered down to the beach with just a pale pink sarong wrapped around her waist, rose-gold round sunglasses, and a big, white, beach hat.

Her body was petite but curvy and she was already tanned. Jake didn't know if it was fake or not, but he couldn't tell either way. Her sandals had a wedge-heel to them, and it added to her swagger.

The pair of them lying next to each other on the beach had looked like a full-on couple, and Jake had to admit they had looked good together.

He'd never had a really close group of friends, and he guessed this must be a taste of what it was like.

In the evening they'd had dinner in their resort, which had been incredible. Tiny lights had been hung all around the pool and the four of them were given a table with a perfect view of the sea.

The food was mouth-watering. Everything was fresh either straight from the sea or off the trees around them

They'd shared a bottle of wine, had a nightcap rum cocktail, which their waiter had recommended and then they'd all disappeared to their own sanctuaries, feeling the jet-lag kicking in.

Jake decided that even if this derailed their focus a little bit he was enjoying himself, and he was just going to go with it.

This was meant to be their adventure after all, and not just about missioning it to get rich. Although, as he surveyed the setting he was currently in, he admitted to himself he wouldn't mind having the means to be able to live like this all the time.

He gazed out at the sand and followed it forward to the sea, looking at the waves rolling in.

His eyes scrolled across the horizon and something caught his eye. "What the fuck."

He stood up, squinting his eyes to get a better look.

The sun wasn't completely up still so the darkness made it harder to see but he was certain there was something there, and it looked like the head of a horse.

"It is the head of a horse," he said out loud, leaning over the railing of his private terrace as far as he could without falling over.

He stood staring for a few more minutes, watching the horse's head bob up and down as it swam out deeper and deeper to the sea.

Then he saw another. And another.

"I must be seeing things." He exhaled deeply. He slipped his feet in to flip-flops and pulled a t-shirt on over his head.

He vaulted over the railing and headed straight for the sea.

The sun was shining more brightly now, and the sea glistened and dazzled him, making him regret leaving his aviators in the apartment.

The sand was a golden-pink colour, the sea was an unnatural turquoise that matched the colour of the little wooden pier slightly further along from them. Now that he was closer, he could clearly see three horses casually swimming in deep water.

He turned to see if anyone else was seeing this, and another horse was being led down to the water by its owner.

"Of course, what else would you do at six in the morning but take your horses for a swim in the sea," Jake mumbled to himself, then walked over to the man.

He smiled, and the man waved and smiled back.

He read Jake's curious and puzzled expression and pointed behind him. "Garrison Savannah race track. These are racing horses," he said.

He stared in stunned amazement at the horses. They were beautiful.

The horse with the man couldn't wait to take a dip and was pulling his trainer closer to the water's edge.

Jake planted himself down on the sand to watch.

There was no one else around, and he wanted to go and wake the others, so they could witness this too, but he was worried by the time he got back the horses would be gone.

He watched the horses swimming powerfully in the sea and back in again for around twenty minutes, while the sun fully came out.

He kicked off his flip flops and dug his toes in to the still cool sand and breathed in the air, it smelled so different here.

Jake had made a real effort to keep some of his wonderment inside because he knew Billy had been to more places than him, and he assumed the girls had too. But to him, it felt like he had landed on another planet.

He looked up and saw the first person that morning aside from the horse trainer.

She was running along the beach, heading towards him, and he could already guess from the graceful strides that it was Issy.

As she got closer, he could make out black shorts and a grey tank top. She had headphones in and was running barefoot.

Her hair was up in a pony-tail that was bobbing up and down with her stride.

With the backdrop of the gleaming ocean, sun, and sand, Jake thought it was quite the sight.

Issy spotted him as she got closer and smiled, slowing down to a light jog. She pulled out her headphones and flopped down next to him.

She was breathing heavily but it was controlled, and while she was sweating a bit, she looked like she could have carried on for hours.

"Well, you don't see that every day," she said, watching the horses as they exited the water. The last horse to go in was just finishing his swim.

"I know, right. I'm already out of words to describe this place and we haven't even been here a full day yet. How was the run?"

"Pretty awesome. I love beach running, and this is some beach. It's beautiful down there. We should go explore a bit today,"

"Sounds good to me," Jake agreed.

They sat in silence, staring out at the now empty expanse of water. Jake felt like he should say something but realized there was no awkwardness. Silence was fine.

They sat for a few more minutes before Issy turned to him and said excitedly, "Breakfast?"

"Yep. Given the state of our apartments, and dinner last night, I cannot wait to see what that's like."

They got to their feet, brushed off some sand, and walked back to the resort.

CHAPTER 13: THE COMPASS

"I'll go and get Amy, you go and get Billy and we'll meet you there in an hour. Grab a table for us," Issy said as they parted ways.

Jake took the few paces from his apartment to Billy's and tapped on the door. It was still pretty early, just after seven now, and he was doubtful Billy would be awake, but he couldn't wait to talk to him about their plans.

"Come in, door should be open," Billy called out.

"Morning, man. How'd you sleep? Just saw the most amazing thing down at the beach."

Billy was shaving in the bathroom but looked like he'd been awake a while.

"Yeh, slept awesome. What did you see?"

Jake told his friend about the horses at dawn, and about Issy turning up after her run.

"Sounds spectacular. That girl sure does have one hell of a body on her," he stated with a laugh.

Jake smiled but was weirded out to find it was forced.

"Ha ha! Don't worry, man. I'm just teasing. The horses sound incredible. I wonder if they do that every day? And good to hear you're getting on with Issy, they're fun to hang out with, right?"

"Yeh, they are. I was actually thinking about that this morning. But, how are we going to explore the island and find our mark without them finding out what we're up to?"

Billy thought back to his conversation on the plane and felt a pang of shame as heat rushed to his face.

"We'll figure it out. Want to go over the Barbados bottle again? You still think the pointy star marking is the one we should hit up first?"

Back in England they'd gone through the markings on each map and made a list.

There was an eight-pointed star on both the map they assumed was Barbados, and the one they thought was Antigua.

There was no pointy star on the third island that remained hidden.

"I think so. It still looks like a compass to me and we've compared it to loads of pictures online.

"It's a bit of a reach but if pirates used compasses for navigation and to find stuff they were looking for then maybe it symbolises that here too. As in, find this point marked by the compass and it'll lead you to the hidden island. Hopefully it's the same deal in Antigua. Like putting the two parts of a jigsaw together to find a third."

"Yeh. That would make sense. I'm just worried it's not that obvious and there's more to it," Jake replied. "And what could we possibly find that's going to magically point us in the direction of some mysterious island that doesn't seem to exist on any map?"

"No idea, but all the other symbols, on these two maps seem to be for landmarks, or stuff that could have been here a long time ago. The compasses aren't landmarks, or we think they're compasses, and possibly not landmarks. They're different," Billy said.

While they'd been talking, Billy had reached for his backpack from the top of his closet, got the bottles out, and set them down in front of them on the floor.

"See. Look. This anchor one could mean there were ships here or some sort of port. These waves could mean the water is choppy, this peak means high ground. We've already tallied that up with Google maps, trees equals, well, trees, and so on. There are a few others, like this one that looks like a sword, and this one that looks like a flaming torch, but I'm thinking we should start with the compass," Billy said as he pointed to the spot on the bottle.

"It's even in bolder ink. Like someone has gone over this carefully a number of times to make sure it stands out, same as on this map too," Jake said and held the Antigua map up to the light from the window.

"Cool sounds good to me, and it's not that far either. Although I guess nothing's that far on this island, which is good for us."

"How did you get on with the boat?" Jake asked.

"It's not that easy to just rent a boat here, and apparently you need some sort of local licence, so I called my mom—which shocked the hell out of her—and pulled in some favours. She's got friends that own a property not far from here, and I guessed they'd have a boat—and I guessed right." He grinned.

Jake smiled as he eyed the bottle then turned to Billy.

"Yea. A fifteen foot boat. We're going to pick up the keys today then we can take it out for a spin and explore a bit of the coastline."

"Awesome. We're really doing this!" Jake said. "What are we going to tell the girls?"

Billy rubbed his chin, nodding. "Well, I was thinking about that. I was doing a bit of research and apparently, it's this thing called Oistins Fish Fry today, happens every Friday and the place just goes off. Huge party."

"Cool. Let's go to breakfast now and tell them we're going to sort out some excursions for the next few days for the four of us, but while we do that they should make the most of the beach and the pool today," Jake added.

"Then we'll be back around later to take them out for the evening, our treat.

"They'll hopefully love the gesture and we're golden, but if they question it we need to be firm and insistent, and also when we bring this up and tell the plan to them we need to be ready to move sharpish, so we can disappear before they ask too much, or worse, invite themselves along."

"Sounds good. I haven't got a better plan." Shrugged Jake.

They carefully returned the bottles to Billy's backpack and went to breakfast.

It was just before eight, so they should be in time to grab a table as Issy suggested.

CHAPTER 14: THE SPLIT

"That was the best breakfast I've ever had," Jake said. "I want to go back again, but round four is probably pushing it?"

"I have no idea where you put it, pretty boy," Amy said, studying Jake's lean physique.

Jake took the last sip of his coffee and looked over at Billy, who nodded subtly.

It was time.

Jake coughed, stood up and stuffed the last bit of toast in his mouth, hoping Billy would lead. He was better at this stuff.

"So, Jake and I have a little surprise for you. We thought we would go organize a few excursions for the four of us over the next few days, and then take you out for dinner later—our treat," Billy stated, with a big smile on his face.

"It's a thing called Oistins Fish Fry tonight and it's a pretty big party on the island, happens every Friday. Great food, music and plenty of rum—sound good?" Jake added.

"Sounds great. I was planning on a swim and then hitting the beach," Issy replied.

Amy's mouth had been open, about to speak and Jake and Billy both suspected she wasn't going to make it as easy for them, but thankfully Issy had given them an opportunity to escape and they'd been backing away from the table even as she was speaking.

"It's a date, pick you up at six," Billy shouted over his shoulder as they took off.

* * *

Amy gave her friend a look.

"What? Oh, come on. You're not still banging on about this treasure stuff? They're just being nice."

"Uh huh, sure they are. I want in, Iss. Are you not the least bit curious? And wouldn't it be much cooler if the headline read, 'Foursome find ancient

Caribbean treasure worth millions?'"

"Yea. Okay. That does sound better. Does that stuff really even exist, though? When does anyone ever find treasure?"

"When they have a map and know where to look. I was doing some searching on the internet last night and there were loads of shipwrecks off this island, and plenty of pirating going on. One bloke put lights in his coconut trees, so ships would think it was the harbour, then when they crashed on the rocks he'd head down and pirate the fuck out of the poor bastards. His house is still on the island over on the east coast. I bet that's where they've gone!"

"Maybe. Let's get it out of them tonight. They seem decent enough. I kinda like hanging out with them."

"Yeh, they're all right, I guess," Amy agreed, with a reluctant smile. "They'll probably try and screw us over at some point, better we do it to them first." She laughed. "I'm joking, I'm joking," she added quickly, seeing her friend's disapproving expression.

"Beach or pool?" Issy asked.

"Pool. Then a light lunch. Beach for a couple of hours then get ready. Plan?"

"Plan," replied Issy.

CHAPTER 15: THE COVE

"Enjoy, and watch out, she's got a kick to her. Bit like your... ah, I mean, have a good time!"

The old boy who loaned them his boat waved them off from the shore as they puttered out to deeper water.

"Uhh. How did this guy know your mum again?"

"I didn't ask, I can probably guess, and I definitely do not want to know," replied Billy, steering them to open water.

"Right. Where we headed?"

"Towards Freyers Well Bay. The compass symbol covered a fair bit of the area but that seems a good starting point," stated Billy, and manoeuvred the boat so they were facing north and started to direct them along the west coast of Barbados.

There was a breeze but no notable wind. The sun was high, and hot.

The air was a little less thick out at sea than it had been on land, and the humidity made the spray from the waves a pleasant sensation.

They passed some bigger settlements of brightly painted boats, all sizes milling around each other. Some with women's names emblazoned on the side in big letters. They spotted an Elinor, an Anna, and a Mandy.

The sea was unlike anything Jake had seen before. It seemed to change colour, flickering different shades of greens and blues.

Jake couldn't see the fish beneath them, and whatever else was down there, but he knew it was there, hidden below the surface.

"I think we're coming up to Freyers Well Bay," Billy said, pointing up ahead.

He slowed the boat down as much as he could, and they gazed along at the coast, wondering if there was actually any secret somewhere here for them to find.

They went along slowly, following the coast around and getting as close as they possibly could. Eyes-peeled, but nothing immediately stood out.

They saw beautiful beaches and a few bays they could possibly explore further.

"Okay. So, that's the last of this bit of coast. Nothing more up this way but open sea ahead and then the north of the island over there. I'll turn her around and we can have another look and maybe stop in a few of those bays we saw," Billy stated.

Jake nodded. "Yeh, good idea. I have no idea what we're looking for but if something is still here it must have been hidden well and not out in plain sight."

Billy turned the boat around and started making their way south down the coast.

They stopped at the first bay they saw, found a place to moor the boat and hopped over the side, splashing in to the shallow water.

"It's not even cold, I can't get over this place. I'm definitely coming back," Jake said.

"Yeh, I know right? Imagine how explorers must have felt the first time they washed up around here," Billy said, as his head turned in all directions, taking everything in. "They must have thought the same thing. I wonder how our pirate felt when he was here, if he was here," corrected Billy.

"I think he was here. I've just got a feeling. I think whoever hid those bottles in that tunnel was hiding something pretty important. They went to a lot of trouble to carve out that secret shelf," said Jake, making his way across a few rocks as if expecting to find a similar hidden shelf here as well.

After a good hour searching the little bay, and when a few tourists and locals started showing some interest, Billy and Jake called time and got back in the boat.

"There was a slightly bigger cove a little further down, if you remember? I reckon we've got time to do a decent search there and then we need to head back."

"I'm guessing we're going to be faced with a barrage of questions. I'm hoping we can distract them with fine food and booze." Billy smirked.

"Ha ha, yeh. That'd work on me."

They were just powering past the Freyers Well Bay daydreaming in the direction of the shore and taking in the alien sights and sounds when Jake stood up in the boat.

"There." Jake lifted his arm and pointed. "What's that?"

Billy pushed his sunglasses on top of his head and strained to make out what Jake was pointing at.

Then he saw it too. "You can't see it straight on, only at this angle... and it's gone again," Billy said. "I'll turn us around."

What they'd seen neither of them were surprised they'd missed the first time around.

High up hidden among the rocks, and only visible from a certain angle, was a dark hole cut in to the side of a jagged outcrop. If the rock-face had been a house, the dark hole looked like a window and it was easily big enough to fit through.

Jake had only spotted it because the sun had happened to shine on something glistening inside, that had caused the cave-like entrance to almost glow, and then, as their boat changed positions and the sun lost its mark it was gone again, and the window had vanished.

Getting inside wasn't going to be easy though.

"How the hell are we going to get up there?" Billy asked. Seeing no obvious place they could secure the boat and no route that would enable them to climb up, even if they could find a spot to leave the boat.

After losing the black window's location, they struggled to find it again even though they were staring hard and thought they knew where to look. They were also wrestling with the sea to avoid hitting land and damaging the boat, which was making things doubly difficult.

"If you were going to hide something so no one would ever find it unless you told them where it was, there would be the place," Jake said out loud, determination and excitement building inside him.

They tried for what felt like an age to either wedge the boat between two bigger rocks below where they thought the cave window was, so one of them could try and keep it moored while the other jumped out to see if there was a way to climb up. But it was no use.

Jake had been very tempted just to dive in the sea and swim up to the bottom of the outcrop of rocks, but the rock surface looked slippery and there were no clear hand-holds.

The waves were also a consideration.

"It's not worth the risk," Billy said. "Our best bet is to mark this spot on the map, moor a bit further along the coast, and then try to reach it by land."

Jake was reluctant to leave now, when he felt they were so close.

To this point their trip had been fantasy for him. A brilliant escapism that was extremely unlikely to result in any big outcome, but one that was well worth taking all the same.

But seeing this had made him believe.

There was something here. Something someone had gone to great lengths to keep hidden a long, long time ago.

And they were so close to finding out what it was.

Billy read his mind. "It's been hidden hundreds of years, man. It will still be hidden tomorrow."

"Let's find the best place to moor and do a practice run. Then we can come back tomorrow fresh and pick up the trail."

They made their way down the coast for another few minutes before finding the little beach both of them agreed would be perfect.

It was pristine, beautiful, and largely deserted.

It was also hidden between the large rocky outcrop containing the secret window they'd just come from and a smaller rocky bit a little further along.

"At least it shouldn't be too hard to find this spot tomorrow now that we know where it is," Jake said.

At the back of the beach, rocks rose high in to the sky forming almost a cliff face, and they guessed they connected with the rocky section they were so keen to conquer. The bay was seemingly unreachable by land and only accessible by water.

A few couples had obviously sought it out by boat themselves for the seclusion and romanticism and looked at the two young lads dragging their boat up on the sand with a combination of curiosity and annoyance.

Billy and Jake took a quick walk around and climbed as high as they could to get the best view in the direction of the secret cave window, but the rocks were too steep, and they didn't get very far.

"I think it's in that direction, and it can't be far from here at all," Billy pointed out.

"I can't see any easy way to get there, but there must be a way."

"Cool. We've made progress. It's actually kind of reassuring it's so difficult. If it was easy, whatever was hidden there would probably have been taken a long time ago," Billy stated in a slight whisper.

"This way, there is a good chance it's still there. "Let's go back to the resort, shower, get changed, and meet the girls," Jake said.

Billy nodded. They headed back to their boat and put it back in the water.

Both were quiet on the drive back, deep in thought.

It felt like they were not here for nothing.

CHAPTER 16: OISTINS

Amy and Issy were sitting in reception, waiting.

Amy pulled her sunglasses down to the end of her nose, so she could peer at Billy and Jake unobstructed as they approached.

She waited until eye-contact had been made, re-adjusted her glasses so they sat firmly on her face again, and continued to look at her phone.

"Hey. How was your day?" Issy asked brightly, just noticing they were there.

"Yeh, it was good. I think we've lined up some really good stuff to do. I mean, you'll like it, a lot, I'm sure," said Billy, hurrying and stumbling over his words.

Jake and Billy had made it back with barely time to spare until they were supposed to meet the girls, having organised exactly zero activities for the four of them to do, and no decent story they could come up with to explain their disappearing act.

"It'll be fine. We'll tell them we met some locals who showed us a bit of the island because they wanted us to see the real Barbados, so we could plan the best shit to do during our stay."

"Oh, yeh, I'm sure they're totally going to buy that."

"Don't worry, man. We don't have to tell them anything. Just let them wonder," Billy said.

They'd hurried to the nearest excursion office, found the most impressive sounding outings, without really knowing what was involved—one was a boat trip and one was in a Jeep on land—and thrown money at the problem.

Rather, Billy threw money at the problem and seeing no other option Jake uneasily went along with it, feeling the anxiety grow along with his, 'I owe you' note.

The sales lady couldn't believe what was happening. The more expensive the excursion she tried to sell them, the more excited, and happy they got.

"Yes! If we return with that there's no way they'll be pissed about being ditched, and far too interested to ask too many questions about today," Billy had said.

They got back to their apartments, showered then threw on some clothes in fifteen minutes flat, and hurried to reception to find their dates.

Jake wasn't sure whether to call it a date, but it felt as much like one as anything he'd ever been on before. So, in his head he was calling it a date, just not out loud. Either way they were here now, for better or worse.

"You look incredible!" Billy beamed at Amy, holding his arms out wide, as if everyone staying in the resort should gather round and admire her.

To be fair, Amy's transformation was eye-catching.

She had looked very attractive in casual clothes, and her bikini had revealed she looked great with barely any clothes, but this was Friday night outfit—and she'd gone to town.

Her tanned legs were stretching out of a khaki green wrap mini-dress and resting crossed on the foot-stool in front of her, she had high-heel wedge sandals with the straps climbing up her calves, bright red lipstick, long fake eye-lashes, and she'd fixed her hair to one side, so it was less natural and messy and more styled.

The final touch was her sunglasses, they were Billy's 80s-style black shades that she either borrowed or pinched from the beach.

"And you look like you got ready in a hurry, so where are you taking us?" Amy asked, her glasses perched on the tip of her nose once more and her feet still firmly up on the footstool in front of her, implying this better be good or they wouldn't be going anywhere.

Issy had already sat up ready to go and was perched on the edge of the stool.

She tried to shuffle herself back a bit to look less eager.

Jake smiled at her, she smiled back and shrugged just enough for Jake to catch it.

Issy looked less formal than her friend but she'd undoubtedly made an effort and Jake couldn't stop staring.

She had a bright, barely worn pair of white trainers on, white short shorts with rips and frays at the edges, and a pale blue V-neck t-shirt with two pockets on the front.

Like Amy, her eyelashes had grown, and gold eye-shadow, red lipstick, it may have even been the same one. Jake couldn't tell. Her hair was down.

Jake subconsciously ran his hand across his head to smooth his untidy mousy blond-brown hair to one side, before trying to smooth out his white shirt that hung loosely and untucked, with the cuffs undone.

He'd found a pair of denim shorts and white shoes and had thrown them on hurriedly.

Billy had done the same. He'd pulled a pair of three-quarter-length black skinny trousers out of his bag, and the first t-shirt that tumbled out with it, a crumpled pale red one with a print of a bear standing up on it. He'd then slipped on a pair of brown boat shoes and rushed for the door.

"Don't worry, we got this," he said, lingering his look on Amy until he saw her thaw a little.

"Shall we?" He offered his hand.

Amy slipped her hand into Billy's.

They led the way and they found a taxi waiting at reception.

Billy got in the front passenger seat, and Amy, Jake, and Issy bundled in to the back, with Amy in the middle as the smallest of the three.

"It gets kinda crazy later on, you'll need this," the driver said to Billy, handing him his card.

"So, this is a big night on the island?" Amy poked her head in between the front two seats.

"Hell yeah. Oistins is it!" The driver beamed.

The others smiled, sat back, and asked him to turn his music up.

"I'm starving," Issy said.

"Don't worry best fish on the island. Shrimp the size of your head! Not far now," the driver said, adding some facts about the island, Oistins, the food, and what they definitely had to do during their stay.

In between listening to their new tour guide, they chatted about what they were going to eat and how hungry they were.

"We haven't eaten since two, we're starving! We had cutters for lunch, it was a sandwich made with salt bread and ham. They were great but that was hours ago!" Issy said, holding her stomach.

"What did you have?" Amy turned to Jake, again pinning her glasses to the tip of her nose and not taking her eyes off him.

He was squirming, and she knew it.

"The guys at the excursion took us for a bit of a drive inland and up the coast so they could point a few things out and tell us some facts about the island, you know? They recommended the best places we could take you. Then they insisted we get some chicken, rice and peas, from this little shack they knew off the beaten track, it was incredible!" Billy's American accent carried loudly from the passenger seat.

Amy hadn't taken her eyes of Jake, and leaned in closer, so her face was inches from his. "Amazing. You said that without moving your lips," she said quietly, before shoving her glasses back in place and returning to her previous position, facing the front.

"This is Oistins, we're here! Like I said, later on gets crazy. Remember to call me and I'll come and get you," reminded the driver.

They thanked him, paid the fare and gave him a tip, before piling out to have a look at their new location.

They were on a main road with people crossing and heading over to their right, so they decided to follow suit.

A few minutes later they were in a maze of canopies and marquee tents turned into bustling kitchens, with queues of eager, hungry punters forming inside each one.

They could see the beach and the sea poking out the other side and wondered if the fish and seafood that was currently on so many barbecues sizzling away, had literally been hauled out mid-swim and flopped on top of each grill.

After exploring a bit more they found the warren of passageways and came out on to one of a few bigger eating areas, with long benches or plastic tables and chairs that were filling up.

They tried to get a closer look at the plates in front of people to see what they were eating. Enormous shrimps, jerk chicken, rice and peas, and mac and cheese seemed to be the most popular.

"Right. Who wants a drink?" Amy asked, bringing them back from their curious fascination with everything around them.

"Two beers?" she asked Jake and Billy, who nodded a thank you. "Issy, beer?"

"Thanks, Ames. Love this place!" she said excitedly, holding her phone away from her and turning so that all of them would be in the picture. A quick snap. "Got it," she said, bringing her phone closer to check the image.

"Billy you're such a dick," she said, laughing.

Amy and Issy were both looking straight at the camera, pouting. Billy was at the back, with a smirk plastered across his face, and Jake's face was screwed up and his mouth was making an 'oooo' shape.

"Good shot, asshole." Jake winced, with his hands between his legs to protect himself from further attacks.

Amy dashed off after the selfie and returned triumphantly a few minutes later with four opened beers.

"Drinks are here!" she announced, handing out the four ice-cold bottles. "That was quick! Good work," said Billy.

"Only a couple of guys in that queue over there and they kindly let me go in front of them." She smiled mischievously.

"Uh huh, I bet they did," said Billy, looking around to try to locate who she was referring to.

Amy was pleased with the reaction.

"Protective much? Or are you a little jealous, Bill?"

He laughed off the question and proposed a toast.

"When Jake and I planned this trip we always thought it would be a one of a kind, we'd look back on and think, 'fuck, that was awesome.' It's pretty safe to say it's living up to expectations. Here's to the rest of our holiday. Cheers."

"Cheers." Amy smiled. "In one." She tipped her bottle high in the air and drank It down in seconds while the others watched, stunned.

"Well!?" Amy demanded, wiping the last drops of cold beer from her lips with the back of her hand.

Issy shrugged and started to drink and the two boys followed suit.

Jake finished his first, Billy finished shortly after, and they turned to wait for Issy.

"Pffffffft!" The bottle fell from her lips still half full, beer fizz escaping from her mouth.

"I'm not much of a drinker, as you can probably tell." She grinned.

"You take your time. I'll get us another round," Billy said as he stood and headed to the bar.

"The food smells amazing. What are you going to have?" Jake ventured, aiming his awkward small talk between Amy and Issy, not making eye contact with either.

"Has to be some jerk chicken, I think. I'm ravenous." Issy took another sip from her bottle, which still had plenty of beer left in it.

"Shrimp for me. How about you, pretty boy?" Amy teased. "You could do with putting some meat on your bones, there's nothing to you." She grabbed his shirt and lifted it up to his chest revealing his toned, flat stomach before he could stop her.

"Yeh, I know, I know. I've never been able to put on weight, I've always been skinny." He shrugged, reaching for a pack of cigarettes and a lighter in his shorts pocket.

Jake watched as her face dropped. She opened her mouth to say something but Issy got in there first.

"Are you kidding me? You've got a better six-pack than me and I train twice a day! I'd kill to have abs like that." She laughed, reaching out to touch his stomach and retreating her hand mid-gesture.

Billy returned with another round of beers.

"What's everyone eating? Want to grab that table over there and I'll go and order a bunch of stuff?"

Jake, glad of the distraction, jumped on the free plastic table and chairs and was quickly followed by the others.

They placed their orders with Billy and sat back, breathing in the sticky air and enjoying any remaining stress and awkwardness leave their bodies as the first couple of beers took hold.

While they waited for their food, they talked around nothing important; the weather, the crowd amassing quickly around them.

There was a real mixture of locals and tourists, largely Americans, and plenty of people were already letting loose and dancing wildly to music pumping from various gigantic speakers dotted around the place.

"We have to dance later," Issy commanded, reaching for her beer.

Jake actually liked dancing but wasn't a fan of being watched while doing so. The thought already making his stomach a little uneasy.

"Absolutely," he replied, kidding no one.

Both girls smiled.

"I'll show you a few moves, don't worry," Issy said with a smirk.

And before Jake had time to find out what that meant, Billy returned with their food and another round of beers.

They ate, drank, and with a few beers now swirling through their bodies, started to have more interesting conversations.

"So how come neither of you have boyfriends, or do you? I can't see any rings at least," Billy asked.

Amy told the story about her ex, how she'd completely fallen for him and now, looking back, couldn't believe that she had.

"He was a complete asshole. How the hell did I not see it?" She choked as some beer went down the wrong way.

She even told them about that night she'd walked in on, and the expression on the other woman's face.

There was a silence while the boys tried to find the right response and then Billy couldn't help it and burst into hysterics, setting all of them off.

"That's like the most awkward thing I've heard in my life, ever!

"What did she do, yank on his ears to get him to stop or let him finish in his own sweet time!?"

"Asshole." Amy crossed her legs, folded her arms, and turned away, but there was a smile at the corner of her mouth that gave away the fact she was actually finding this exchange amusing, and surprisingly therapeutic.

"How about you, Issy? Any exes you'd rather forget?"

"One or two," she said, looking at her bottle. She took a large mouthful of beer, then swallowed it before replying. "I've been playing football for most of my life and it takes up so much time."

She smiled. "There's still not that much money in women's football, yet. It is changing and the progress in the last few years has been awesome, but the contracts are obviously way off the men's game. I used to work second jobs but at least now I'm professional and playing for a big club, I don't have to do that anymore. I can just concentrate on my game and being as good as I can be."

She took the last sip and emptied her bottle of beer. "I wouldn't change it for the world but hasn't left a lot of time for dating.

"And the guy's I have dated have never really got on board with the fact I have to get up early for training or matches, you know? They just want to go out and get wasted because that's what everyone else our age is doing."

"Their loss, right?" Jake smiled at her and looked around at Billy and Amy for support.

"Hells yeah. Have you seen this girl?" Amy grabbed her friend's hand and then pulled her towards the bar.

"We're getting more drinks, time for some rum," Amy shouted over her shoulder.

"Sure," Billy shouted back.

He turned to Jake. "Issy's definitely in to you," he said and sat back smiling expectantly at Jake, as though he'd asked a question.

"Really? It's so hard to read her… and..."

"Ah, come on. You think so too. I can tell you like her."

Jake looked over to the queue to see where they were and saw Issy and Amy joking around with two guys.

Issy was already moving a little in time with the bass from the nearest speaker. Amy looked her usual confrontational self.

"I dunno man," was all he could manage. Billy shook his head and laughed.

"Well, when I make a move on Amy, and I'm going to, it'll be just the two of you. What's your plan then, dude?"

"As if you'll… yeh, okay, let's just cross that bridge when we come to it."

The girls had been served and returned with four plastic cups.

"Rum!" Issy explained, holding out the four cups so Jake and Billy could take one.

"I'm pretty sure I saw some sort of dance floor and a stage over that way. Come on, let's go," Issy said.

"A stage!?" Jake mouthed to his friend, the anxiety shooting through his body.

Billy just shrugged and smiled, necking his drink and dumping the empty on the table before getting up and following the two girls, who were getting plenty of attention from surrounding eyes.

Issy looked around to see where Jake was, and realising he hadn't budged far from his plastic chair, leapt back to his side, grabbed his arm and dragged him with them, not taking no for an answer.

"Don't worry, I got you," she leaned in and whispered in his ear.

Jake felt himself going red but was pretty sure no one could see.

The rabbit warren maze opened itself out in to a still-covered clearing, rapidly filling with bodies.

They were all facing in one direction.

Jake looked round to see the thing he'd been dreading, the stage, which currently was occupied by two girls and a guy, seemingly local, doing what he could only describe as body-popping.

They weren't wearing much, and he could see every muscle and fleshy part rhythmically vibrating to the bass and the beat.

"Wow, how the hell are they doing that?" he said, hoping Issy would engage in conversation and drop the stage dancing idea.

But she was bouncing in time herself, staring wide-eyed at the jiggling and limb-vibrating going on in front of her.

She started copying the girl on stage, sticking her ass out behind her and moving her body in almost exactly the way they were.

Fuck it, thought Jake, accepting there was no way out of this situation, he started dancing too.

"Yeaaaah, woooooo!" Amy yelled, spotting them and drawing the attention of the still growing crowd.

Jake realised he needn't have worried so much as all eyes were on Issy, who's moves were even outshining the two girls and the guy still on stage.

Amy cheered them on, and Billy stood watching open-mouthed along with many others in the crowd.

Eventually the song changed and Issy, sweating slightly, took the opportunity to take a break.

"Drink?" she asked in Jake's ear.

He nodded numbly, still trying to process what had just happened.

Issy grinned and winked at him disappearing towards one of the stalls, with Jake's eyes, and the eyes of almost all the men in the marquee following her figure as she walked away.

"Woah, that was fucking insane." Billy came up to him with Amy in tow.

"Yeh, I know right? I'll go and help her with the drinks."

"Where the hell did you learn to dance like that?" Jake asked, joining her one from the front of the queue.

Issy was still moving her hips slightly side to side.

"My best friend from school is Jamaican, she taught me a few moves." She giggled.

"Yeh, she did! What we getting?"

"I was thinking more of those rum punch things, and some shots! Tequila?"

"Fuck, I hate tequila."

"Tequila it is." She snickered, jumping up to the bar and ordering before Jake could stop her.

"Let's do ours here. Look there's some salt." She grabbed a shaker from a nearby table, licked her bare arm and sprinkled salt over the wet patch.

Jake then did the same.

They picked up their shot glasses and made eye-contact. "Cheers, Jake. On three…"

Jake had forgotten all about his awkwardness and wasn't worried about what he was going to say next anymore. All he could think about now was how he was going to make a move.

"THREE!"

Jake jumped and quickly lifted the glass to his face, getting half of the liquid in his mouth and the rest over his chin and neck.

Issy knocked hers back in one shot but the taste and strength of the alcohol caused her to screw her face up and squeeze her eyes tight shut.

"You missed a bit," she said and leaned in towards him, stole a quick glance at his expression, then quickly licked the tequila off his neck.

She pulled away and smiled.

Jake was speechless, and just grinned.

"Come on give me a hand," Issy said, grabbing two of the rums and tequilas and with a nod of her head to Jake suggesting he should do the same.

They returned to the dance floor to find Billy and Amy dancing tightly together.

Jake was surprised to see Amy was somewhat of a self-conscious and awkward dancer, but Billy was taking the lead.

With Billy a tall, dark, and somewhat contrary partner in his off-red bear t-shirt they made a striking couple.

"Get a room." Issy laughed, handing her friend one of the plastic cups. Jake handed a drink to his friend.

"Cheers." He held up his drink and they held their cups together.

"How about we take a breather over there?" Amy asked, pointing to a plastic table with four chairs in a corner that had recently been vacated.

"Good idea, I'll grab the table," Issy said, striding off in its direction.

When they were all settled they took a moment to have a look at what was going on around them. The crowd had grown massively and become way more lively.

"It's so weird, isn't it? This island seems so chilled—and then this!" Billy laughed.

"So, what's the plan for tomorrow boys? Where are you taking us?" Amy asked, looking at Jake expecting him to cave first.

"Yes! What's the plan? Can we come with you tomorrow and help you find the treasure?" Issy chipped in eagerly, the beers, rum, and shots taking their toll on someone not used to drinking.

A deafening silence followed despite the reggae din in full swing around them.

Jake's face turned from Issy, to Amy, and finally to Billy.

"You… you told them?"

"I didn't tell them everything, I just…"

"Oh, good, lies. My favourite. So, what did you tell us Billy, and what did you leave out?" Amy asked, the mood souring.

"Oh, shit. I'm sorry, I just thought…" Issy tried but she knew she'd put her foot in it. The alcohol had ruined the moment.

More silence.

Billy decided to try and placate Jake first.

"I'm sorry, man. I had a few too many on the plane and told Amy about the bottles… and the maps," he stated.

"What the fuck? I can't believe this. If you're gonna share that shit, don't you think you should consult me first? What we found, discovered, could be huge. It could be game-changer stuff, and you told someone that you had *just* met!"

"It's not like that… I–"

"Hang on. I thought you said he inherited them? I see it's not just me you've been lying to," Amy stated and folded her arms across her chest.

"What's wrong with telling us anyway?" Issy asked, looking hurt.

Jake looked around the table, frustration reaching boiling point.

"Well, this is an absolute shit-show. Nice work, mate." He snatched up his drink and got up from the table.

"Come on, man, it's no big deal. I'm sorry. Let's finish our drinks and we'll figure it out," Billy pleaded.

Jake went to say something then stopped himself.

"I'll see you later," was all he could manage before storming off towards the beach.

The three of them sat buzzing from the alcohol and desperate to say something but stunned in to silence.

"So, I'm guessing, pretty boy's got some good reasons to be that upset, huh?"

Billy sighed, shook his head. "I fucked up."

"No, shit. What's going on?" Issy asked impatiently, fidgeting in her seat. "Should I go after him?" she added.

"We found these maps, on the labels of some seriously old rum bottles, I mean by complete and utter chance, in some ancient fucking tunnels underneath this pub in Bristol, in England," Billy said, ignoring the question.

"The pub, and the tunnels, were used by pirates back in the day to ferry their stash secretly to their ships in the docks. It's a long story how we ended up in there, but we found a hidden compartment in one of the tunnels, with a metal box in it and the bottles inside that. The bottles have maps on them, and we figured whoever put them there must have had a good reason for doing so and must have been trying to keep something pretty valuable, very secret."

The girls were both listening intently.

"It took us a while to figure out where they were maps of, but we think Barbados is one of the maps."

He waited, expecting a barrage of questions but when none came, he continued.

"Another map, we think is Antigua, and the third… we don't know. But there are markings on the first two maps that we think, we hope, if we find them and do a bit of detective work, will tell us where the third island is."

"And what's on the third island?" asked Amy, leaning in closer.

"We haven't figured that out yet. But the bottles and the maps seem legit. They're probably worth a fair bit on their own, but…"

"You think there's some sort of treasure on the hidden island," Issy finished.

"Yeh, pretty much. It could be nothing…"

"But it could also be worth an absolute fucking fortune, I knew it!" Amy finished.

"Yeh."

"We won't tell anyone," Issy offered. "Jake's totally right to be pissed. You found a potentially life-changing discovery and you blurted it out to some girl you'd just met on a plane because her tits caught your eye."

"Idiot," Amy blurted.

"Pretty much," Billy agreed.

"Well, now we know, and I want in. But you need to square things with Jake first," Amy told him firmly.

"Amy…"

"Iss, we're a part of this now whether they like it or not, Jake knows it. Nothing bad has happened. Not really. This idiot has just royally fucked up how it's happened. Same outcome ultimately. And now he's going to fix it." She stared hard at Billy.

He slumped back in his plastic chair and almost caused it to tip over.

Silent for a minute, he then said, "The thing is, he's not going to want to see me right now. But, you…" he turned to Issy.

She opened her mouth to protest but Amy gave her a look and stopped her.

"Can't believe I'm actually saying this—but, he's right," Amy added.

"What! Why me?"

"Because he's got a thing for you, it's so obvious."

Issy had no doubt it was true but remained quiet.

"He's been following you around like an awkward, admittedly quite attractive, dog."

Another pause.

"You think he's on the beach?"

They both nodded.

"What do I say to him?"

"Tell him I'm an ass and I'm sorry. I'm gonna tell him myself. Me and Amy will head down shortly after you, right?" He looked to Amy for confirmation. She nodded.

"I can go now but he was properly fucked off, and I get it. This was our thing, and for Jake this is his big chance to really do something with his life. He's my best friend but he'll tell you himself he's a bit of a dreamer. He's never really had much of a plan and I know he sees this as his big chance…" Billy tailed off, sighing. "Man, I really screwed up."

"Don't worry he'll come around. You're an idiot, but you didn't mean to fuck him with what you did. You were just a bit, you know, both feet first and he knows that," Amy said.

"Go on, Iss. He won't be angry at you."

"Let me go see if I can find him. You guys follow me down in about fifteen minutes, okay?"

They agreed, and she set off in the direction Jake had disappeared.

*   *   *

The party had spilled across the sand and there were people splashing around in the sea.

Issy looked left and right, deciding to head left as it looked quieter, and that was where she would have gone if she was in the same situation.

It was slow going with the sand eating her trainers up with every footstep, so she decided to take them off and go barefoot.

The ground was cool and felt amazing against the soles of her feet and between her toes. She looked out at the dark expanse of water and realised she was more than a bit tipsy.

I won't go further than those lights, she thought, looking along the beach again.

After ten minutes she spotted a dark, hunched figure sitting near the shoreline.

Issy couldn't make out much detail at this stage but she was sure it was Jake and took it as a good sign that he hadn't gone too far and that he wanted, even if it was subconsciously, for someone to go after him.

As she got closer she lost all doubt as she saw his white shirt flapping in the breeze, and his short hair back to its more familiar bed-head state.

"Hey," she offered, falling down on the sand next to him clumsily.

"Hey," he replied.

Jake appeared much calmer now and Amy and Billy had been right, he definitely wasn't angry at her and, she may have been reading too much into his expression, but he even looked a little bit happy she'd come and not the others.

"You okay?"

"Yeh, I'm okay. Sorry I blew up back there. It was really stupid. I've built this trip up way too much in my head. I just kind of felt a bit, I dunno, betrayed, I guess, but I know that's ridiculous." He stared at his feet.

"That's not ridiculous at all. Billy knows he shouldn't have said anything to Amy. He feels really bad," she stated.

Jake looked at her face and saw she was telling the truth.

He'd worried they'd all been laughing at his reaction, and the fact he'd stormed off.

Billy never got too highly strung and always seemed to adapt to new situations easily. He assumed Billy would think he should just chill out.

That he'd also misjudged his friend added to his embarrassment.

"It's probably nothing. It's a few old bottles we found in a pub cellar. We don't even know exactly how old they are, or if the maps are genuine."

He was thankful it was dark, and they were far enough from the lights that Issy couldn't see the reddening of his face.

Jake now knew that once he'd allowed himself to believe there was some sort of treasure, that it might exist, and they just needed to uncover it, he had hoped this trip was going to change his life forever.

Now, he just felt like a fool.

"But you said they matched up with this island? And Antigua, didn't you? The maps? Must have been a pretty close match for you to jump on a plane?"

He paused, thinking about the specific landmarks that had left no doubt in their minds before they'd left England.

"Yeh, they did. The edges were a little off but things like big bays, or high points, and trees and forests all matched up perfectly."

"Then it sounds like you're on to something to me. Something that's definitely worth seeing through at least. It takes some balls to pay all this money and actually do something about it, rather than wondering for the rest of your life what's out there, or letting someone else get all the glory," Issy said.

Shit, the money... Jake thought. Billy had basically paid for everything, and even though Jake was doing his best to keep track of all that he owed they both knew he wouldn't be able to pay it all back.

"So, you don't think we're crazy?"

"Nope, I think it's pretty cool. But I also totally get it if you don't want me and Amy to be involved. This is your thing, go find your treasure." She smiled at him, put both her arms around one of his and rested her head on her shoulder, suddenly feeling exhausted.

"I don't normally drink." She laughed.

Jake looked at his feet again. Behind him and over to the right was probably the best party he'd ever been to, and he had a stunning blonde girl clinging to his arm.

He didn't have a close group of mates that hung out together all the time. Billy was his best friend, and now that he was able to stop and reflect, he couldn't remember, aside from his childhood, ever being quite so happy, or full of purpose.

"Na. We're in this together. The four of us. You're not getting out of it that easily." He grinned at Issy as she looked up at him.

She smiled back and the moment, that felt like it was destined to turn into something more, ended instantly when he heard Amy's voice carrying from further along the beach.

"There they are!" she shouted.

She started running over towards them Billy following just behind.

"We got worried. After you left we realised letting you go off alone in the dark was pretty dumb, sorry Iss."

Issy stood up and Amy jumped on her friend, hugging her. "Don't worry, I'm fine. And Jake's fine too."

They both looked over to where Jake was now standing, brushing off loose sand from his shorts.

Billy walked over to him. "Hey, man, I'm sorry."

"It's all good. I overreacted," he said quietly, embarrassed.

"I promise, I won't say another word to anyone. This is a big deal, man. We're on to something and I'm a hundred percent in from now on," he said.

Then Billy lowered his voice.

"I kind of let the cat out of the bag, though, and I don't think Amy's going to drop it but whatever you want to do, I'm with you. They're awesome but this is our discovery and–"

"It's cool, mate. I was speaking to Issy and thinking about the last few days and it's been great, even better with them here. I told Issy we're all in this together now, the four of us." Jake smiled.

Billy stumbled in the sand. "Really? You sure?"

"Yeh, sure."

Billy grinned. He put an arm around Jake's shoulder and turned to face the others.

"Well, boys and girls, looks like we've got ourselves a foursome!"

"Excellent. We're stuck with you for our whole holiday," Amy mocked with fake sarcasm.

"Come on. Bring it in, bring it in. Hands in the middle."

Issy played along and put her hand on top of Billy's.

"You're such a dick." Jake laughed, eventually putting his hand down on top of Issy's.

"Come on, Amy, it's this or spit handshakes, your call." Billy pretended to be serious and the others laughed.

"Fine." She put her hand on top of Jake's. "What now?"

"Now, we make a pact. I fucked up, but it turned out to be the best fuck up I've made in a while and now added two to our group. No doubt Issy's going to bring her athleticism and smarts to the group, Amy will keep our spirits up with her constant sarcasm…Ow! Kidding, kidding." He rubbed his shin where Amy had knocked it.

"But, we might not get so lucky next time. Full disclosure between the four of us. We pool our resources and find some shiny stuff worth millions, but we don't let on to another living soul." He eyed them all. "Deal?"

"Deal," Issy and Jake agreed.

There was a pause and all eyes turned to Amy. "Deal! Obviously. Jeez you guys are all so dramatic!" She smiled at them.

"Awesome, let's go get a drink." Billy broke the pact by pushing his arm up from the bottom of the pile and forcing everyone else to do the same.

They turned and started walking back towards the music.

CHAPTER 17: DRINKING

When they returned to the party, they managed to find a table and picked up where they'd left off.

Now, however, there was only one thing any of them wanted to talk about.

"Tell us everything. Start from the beginning about how you found these bottles, and then tell us what you found out, and what these maps actually mean," Amy asked, clearly excited.

"This requires more booze. Jake give me a hand, the queue's massive now. Let's get a few drinks each so we don't have to queue up again for a while."

After fifteen or so minutes Billy and Jake returned with a jug of punch for the girls and a pitcher of beer for themselves.

"That should keep us going for a while." Billy grinned, placing the punch on the table in front of Issy and Amy.

Billy and Jake then recounted their story in its entirety. Every time Jake missed out a detail, Billy would jump in to add the missing elements, and when Billy forgot something, Jake picked up the story again.

"We don't know what the strange markings are, but we do know that the two compass symbols are different to the others. They're drawn in bolder ink and more prominent."

"Plus, it's the only marker that features on two of the three maps, and if they are compasses we reckon that's to symbolise that if we find whatever is at these two marks, it will help us navigate our way to the third island, and then we can start to decipher those symbols," Jake added.

"Yeh, we haven't paid anywhere near as much attention to the third map because we didn't see much point until we have some idea of where it is, if indeed it actually exists at all," Billy finished.

They were all up to date now. Well, almost up to date. "Can we see them?" Amy asked.

"Oh, yes, I'd love to see them," Issy agreed.

Jake and Billy glanced at each other and the look was understood by both.

They'd made a pact and agreed to full disclosure and letting Issy and Amy get their hands on the bottles was part of the deal.

"Sure, I don't see why not. It is getting late though, and we've drunk an entire ship's supply of alcohol in one night, maybe come around after breakfast tomorrow and we can study them properly then?"

"No way! Can't we see them now? Let's get a taxi back to the resort and have a nightcap while we have a look," Amy stated, wiggling in her chair.

"We can study them again tomorrow if we need to. Please?" Issy said.

Amy gave Billy her most persuasive pleading look, and Issy stared with a bright smile at Jake.

"Yeh, of course, no worries. I just thought you guys might be tired or whatever.

"That's settled then, let's do it."

Billy slowly got to his feet and felt a slight headrush from sitting down for so long and drinking so much. The others seemed to experience the same sensation as they got out of their chairs too.

"Let's go find us a taxi."

* * *

It was half past eleven by the time they pulled up to Island Spa. "Shall we get something to drink from the bar?" asked Amy.

"Yeh, let's get some ice, and a mixer, and see if we can get a bottle of rum or vodka or something."

"Wait... we could just drink the rum we have in Billy's apartment?" Amy floated the idea as it came to her.

"What rum? We don't... Oh." Jake stopped, comprehending what she was suggesting.

There was a reluctance on all sides to devalue one of their prize assets by drinking its contents, but curiosity and excitement won out and no one, not even Jake, objected.

"I wonder if it's even drinkable? Best get a few beers or something from behind the bar along with the ice and mixer, maybe one sweet like a coconut or pineapple juice, and then just some sparkling water if they have all that, if not grab whatever's available."

"Will do. Come on, Iss," Amy said and took her friend's hand and dragged her off to get the supplies.

"We'll see you in Billy's apartment in ten."

Jake and Billy made their way along the little path in the opposite direction towards where they were staying.

"Is this a good idea? We're going to kick ourselves if those bottles are worth a fortune with their contents intact and basically worthless if not," Jake said out loud.

"Probably not, but neither was knocking a big hole through a wall in an historic pub, but that's worked out pretty well so far."

"Yep, true. This all started with a 'fuck it' and I'm not sure having overly cautious adventurers would really work. Nothing was ever discovered by playing it safe," Jake added.

Billy put his key in the door and let Jake in first. He closed and locked it carefully behind him, then walked to the closet where he'd stashed the bottles in his backpack on the top shelf.

He reached inside the backpack and pulled them out one by one. They were each individually wrapped in Billy's clean t-shirts to give the bottles a bit of protection, should the cleaner accidently pull his bag down suddenly.

Ideally, they'd have put the bottles in the apartment safe along with their passports, but they were too big and didn't fit.

Billy handed one swaddled bottle to Jake to unwrap and he made a start on a second one.

"I've got Barbados," Jake said, holding his bottle aloft making its content gleam gold in the room light.

"And I've got Antigua. Which must make this…" Billy unwrapped the third bundle. "The hidden island."

They carefully lined the three bottles up on the table in front of them, making sure the map labels were all facing the same way for effect.

Neither of them wanted Issy and Amy to come over and be massively underwhelmed and question what they'd been making such a fuss about.

As if on cue there was a rhythmic knock at the door, the girls had arrived.

"Hey, you ready for us? The big unveiling," Amy joked, carrying a bucket full of ice, a bottle of some sort of fruit juice, a bottle of coke, a bottle of sparkling water, and some proper glasses from the bar.

"Well, I didn't think we should drink something so special from plastic beakers or tea cups, or whatever other crockery that's lying around in here."

Her sentence ended abruptly and quietly as she and Issy spotted the bottles on the table at the same time.

They walked over to the table to get a better look. "Can I pick one up?" asked Issy.

"Of course. Have a proper look. They're pretty cool, right?" Jake said.

"They're amazing," Amy said. "You can tell they're old bottles, but you'd never think they were that old."

"When do you think these were hidden away at that pub?" Issy asked.

"We don't know for sure, but we guess around three-hundred years ago. So, they've aged pretty well, considering," Jake replied.

Amy and Issy picked up a bottle each. Issy had the Barbados bottle and Amy was studying the Hidden Island bottle.

Issy's mouth was open, in awe. "These maps are beautiful. It's incredible the lines are still so clear; the drawings are amazingly well done. And the bottles themselves are so cute."

"I can't imagine all rum was put into such fine containers in those days," Amy said, already pointing out something neither Billy nor Jake had paid any attention to.

They sat on the sofa, studying in silence for another ten minutes. "I think you're right about the compasses," Issy said.

"They do look different. Like more care has been taken when drawing them in, and like you said, looks like the lines have been gone over many times. Whereas that's not the case with the rest of the maps. Some parts look like they've faded away."

Another thing Billy and Jake had missed.

"Which parts?" Jake asked, sitting down next to Issy and staring hard at the bottle to try and see what she was talking about.

"There." She pointed a manicured, crème-coloured nail over what looked like a smudge at the edge of the Barbados map, somewhere off the west coast.

"Look closer," Issy encouraged, sensing Jake's frustration and annoyance at himself for missing what could be a key detail.

"I see it. I don't know what it is exactly, but you're right—there was definitely something there and now it's faded over time."

None of them could figure out what it was, aside from two or three wavy lines and a gap where they guessed a drawing used to be.

"Right. Those are some mighty impressive bottles, boys. Which one are we drinking? Amy asked.

"I think it makes most sense to drink Barbados first, you know? It's the first island we've visited and if we hadn't come here we'd have never met you girls, so it seems fitting we toast with Barbados," Jake said.

"Well said, man. Barbados it is. I'm going to take this in the kitchen to try and perform some pretty precise surgery on the seal to try and avoid any damage."

While Billy was doing that, Amy organised four glasses with ice for each of them, and more ice in the middle of the table in case anyone wanted extra.

She also arranged the mixers in the middle, along with crisps in little bowls.

"We should do this in style," she explained, sensing that Issy and Jake were watching her.

Once the table had been arranged, the three of them sat in a row on the sofa with Issy in the middle, waiting impatiently but quietly so as not to stress Billy.

They preferred he return with a fully intact but open bottle of Barbados rum, from circa sixteen-hundred-and-something.

"Got it!" Billy's voice boomed from the kitchen, coinciding with the two doors to the terrace slamming shut hard, making an almighty bang that scared the life out of the three sitting close to the doors.

"Wow. Wind's really picking up out there. Must be a storm coming," Jake said, jumping up to make sure there was no damage, and to secure the doors properly so it didn't happen again.

"Sounded like some positive sounds from the kitchen though?" Jake half-shouted over his shoulder to get confirmation from Billy that he had opened the first bottle.

He looked out the window and saw the palm trees swaying violently and bending over almost horizontally in one direction, before snapping back to their original position after a few seconds.

"Huh," he said puzzled. "Wind seems to have settled down again, the weather over here is nuts."

He bolted the doors, just in case, and was about to go and inspect Billy's handiwork when his friend appeared with a huge smile on his face, holding an open bottle aloft.

"The wax seal was the tricky part. That was a nightmare to get off without smashing the bottle. Incredibly the cork underneath was not only in one piece, but it came out with a corkscrew as easy as you like. And it doesn't smell half bad either," he added, holding the bottle underneath each of their noses in turn so they could smell for themselves.

"It's definitely spiced," said Jake. "Smells incredible. I've not come across anything like it."

"I have no idea how it'll taste though, or if it's even drinkable but let's give it a go," said Billy.

Jake lined up the glasses Amy had brought from the bar to make it as easy for Billy to pour four equal measures and not spill any.

The glass panes and window shutters in the apartment rattled again as Billy was pouring but not as violently as the gust that had blown through a minute ago.

"Must be passing," Jake said, again looking with a furrowed brow out the window.

He didn't know why but this stop-start storm made him uneasy, he'd never seen wind act in such an unnatural manner, and he thought of their boat and hoped it would come out of whatever this was unscathed.

When Billy was happy with the quantities he added a few big ice cubes to each glass and passed them round.

No one added any mixers, they all wanted to find out how it tasted on its own first.

"A toast." Billy stood in front of them and raised his glass. "Just think. There isn't a single man or woman left alive who can tell you how this rum tastes, and seemingly no one even knows it exists. Here's to finding far more that's been long-forgotten. Cheers!" he said, ending on a lighter note and raising his glass to his lips.

The others did the same, all of them taking a big sip.

As the fiery liquid hit the back of his throat, at first, he couldn't work out what happened.

At almost the exact same time as the four of them drank, the wind howled and smashed through the doors Jake had bolted, this time bringing with it buckets of water from what must have been a sudden tropical downpour.

Issy jumped up and screamed, her glass dropping from her hand and smashing to the floor.

Billy and Jake leapt up to push the doors back in place but found it tough going against considerable force driving at them from outside.

But Amy didn't move.

She looked completely oblivious to the torrent of wind and rain, hurling her hair around and soaking her wet through with its spray.

Jake swore he even saw her take another big sip of the rum, which had tasted as old as time itself, full of oak and spice, and something else he couldn't quite identify.

He wanted more, and he told himself as soon as they sorted out the bloody windows, he'd be topping himself up for sure.

"That blast actually ripped the bolts from the wood in the floor!" Jake exclaimed.

They managed to get one back in, pressed the other up against the frame, and stuck some furniture behind them, so they would stay in place, until tomorrow when they could ask at reception to fix it.

Jake sat back down with his drink and reached for the bottle.

He poured Issy a fresh measure, in a china tea mug this time, then gave himself a generous top up.

He looked around to see if anyone else needed topping-up and saw that Billy had almost finished his, and Amy was completely dry.

"Good stuff this, right?" He laughed.

They all nodded and voiced their agreement. They also agreed there was another strong flavour, but no one could put their finger on what it was.

By the time they said goodnight and parted ways, the bottle was pretty empty.

CHAPTER 18: INSOMNIA

Amy sat upright on her bed.

"Come on, Amy, see if you can get some sleep,' Issy said, climbing under the covers. "I've put the bin from the bathroom next to your bed in case you need to puke."

"I don't feel sick, I'm just not ready to sleep," she said quietly, a million thoughts racing through her head.

"That's just the rum talking," said Issy. "I don't think I've ever drunk that much in my entire life. Tomorrow's going to be interesting. Beach day, I think."

Amy smiled a distant smile and returned to her thoughts. She was scheming.

"It is the rum," she said. "But not in the way you think, Issy. I know what I need to do now. I'm going to find the first compass." She looked in the mirror and was surprised by how dark her eyes were.

"No time to get scared of your own reflection, Amy," she mumbled to herself.

She continued with her thought process. Her brain driven to find the answer to a question she had, prior to tonight, no idea she'd wanted to know so badly.

"That's where they were yesterday—they still hadn't told us even at Oistins—and they must have been close to discovering something. They were gone for hours and if they hadn't found a thing they wouldn't have been so happy when they finally returned. The compass was on the north western edge of the island and the marker was partly in the sea. They must have gotten a boat from somewhere, sailed up the coast, and run out of time as they got close to discovering the thing they'd set out to find."

Amy surprised herself with the speed with which her brain was mapping out her path to the compass. She looked over at Issy.

Her mouth was open, and she was snoring softly, dead to the world.

With Issy's objections no longer a problem, Amy's plotting and scheming rumbled on unrestrained.

CHAPTER 19: THE SEDUCTION

Billy couldn't sleep.

Jake had left with the others and Billy had drank some water and gone through his usual before bed routine.

But his head was buzzing. He couldn't relax and felt agitated, as if he should be doing something but he didn't know what it was.

His phone buzzed on the bedside table next to him. He picked it up and looked at the glowing screen.

It was a text—from Amy.

His heart raced immediately, and his first thought was that something had happened.

She'd been acting really strange towards the end of the night, ever since they had the rum.

The rum. Maybe it hadn't been drinkable after all. Maybe they'd all managed to poison themselves. But spirits didn't go bad, did they?

He opened the message and almost dropped his phone, his heart racing even more.

It was a picture, of Amy, but not how he'd ever seen her before.

She was standing in hers and Issy's bathroom. She still had her wrap-around green dress on, but she was leaning on her elbows bending over towards the mirror in front of her, posing and biting her lower lip.

Her right hand was holding her phone and pointing the camera at the mirror, and her left hand was reaching down to her side, balling up the material and forcing the dress to ride up higher, revealing her bare thigh and a bit more in the reflection in the second mirror, which was mounted on the wall directly behind her.

The strap had also fallen down her left arm revealing the top of her black bra and plenty of cleavage.

It was the most seductive picture Billy had seen. She'd given him a three hundred and sixty degree view. He couldn't stop staring.

Underneath the picture she'd simply written: *Can I come over?*

There was just one thing that disturbed him, Amy's eyes. Her pupils were so big and black, he couldn't quite put his finger on it, but her expression was unnatural and unnerved him a bit.

Or maybe that's just how she looked when she was horny. Either way, he typed a message back. One word: *Yes*

He quickly leapt off the bed and went to brush his teeth and tidy himself up a bit before she arrived.

He added some aftershave and was about to re-position himself on the bed when there were three distinct knocks.

Before he'd even fully opened the door, Amy breezed in and pounced on him, pushing him back on the bed and kissing him full on the mouth.

She kissed him for a good minute until she knew it was having the desired effect then she jumped up, shut the door, then rolled her dress up over her body and dropped it unceremoniously on the floor, leaving her standing in just black underwear. The same simmering expression from the picture still in her eyes.

"Wow," was all Billy could manage.

"Get undressed," she ordered him, without raising her voice.

Billy was almost certain this was part of some act and she was playing a character.

He went with it, took his clothes off, apart from his boxers, and lay on the bed.

"This is what you get for ditching us and going on a boat trip without us." She slid her body over his and shimmied up, straddling his chest.

"How did you... that was before, though. That wouldn't happen again after tonight because–"

"Give me your arm." She pointed to his left arm.

Billy did as he was told, worried that if he acted up at all she'd get offended he rejected her roleplay, or whatever this was.

Amy produced the sarong she was wearing at the beach from her bag that she'd dropped by the side of the bed.

Billy couldn't take his eyes off her body as she proceeded to tie his arm to the bed with the sarong.

"Now the other one." She pulled another sarong from her bag, and kissed his hand then pressed it to the headboard and tied it as well. She gave the knot one final tug to check it was secure, and satisfied that it was, moved to the next step.

So far, so good, she thought, catching a glimpse of some loose change on the dresser, hoping it had what she needed.

"Now, close your eyes." She wiggled down his body and kissed him on the lips.

Billy had closed his eyes for the kiss and just as he re-opened them he saw the blackness of a sleeping mask steal away his vision as it slid over his head.

Once that was secured, Amy whispered in his ear, "I'll be back in two minutes. I'm going to the bathroom. Just think about all the things I'm going to do to you while I'm gone." She slid off of him and off the bed, found the remote to the sound-system and turned on the radio, as loud as she thought she could get away with, without it being too suspicious.

She then opened the bathroom door, turned on the tap, and closed the door with her still on the outside, tiptoeing so Billy would, with a bit of luck, think she was in the bathroom.

Next, she grabbed one of the dining chairs, put it next to the closet, hoisted herself up on the chair, reached in the back of the closet, fetching the three bottles, one, of course, now empty.

She kept them wrapped in Billy's t-shirts so when she put them in her bag they wouldn't clink around.

Finally, and here's where she really hoped she'd guessed right and had luck on her side otherwise the whole thing could unravel. She walked over to the dresser where she'd spied the loose change and, seeing that she had been right, grabbed the keys to Billy's boat.

With everything she came for safely in her bag now slung across her shoulder, she picked her dress up off the floor, tucked it under one arm, gave a quick glance at Billy to make sure he hadn't found her out yet, slipped her shoes on and marched out in to the night in her underwear.

CHAPTER 20: THE CHASE

Billy had followed the instructions to the letter and had been daydreaming about what was to follow.

Finally, his brain jolted into life and he sensed that some time had passed. "What the hell is she doing?" he asked out loud.

"Amy, you okay in there?" he yelled. No reply.

He tried to pull his right arm free but was surprised to find he'd been tied up a lot more securely than he'd been expecting.

He tugged at the left arm without any more success. "AMY?" he yelled louder, starting to freak out. "What the actual fuck?"

He wrestled with the sarongs for a good fifteen minutes before he felt one of them start to loosen.

Another couple of minutes and his right arm was free. He immediately ripped off the sleeping mask and squinted as his eyes adjusted to the light.

Nothing. He could still hear the tap running in the bathroom over the radio but all else was silent, and no sign of Amy.

He panicked and fumbled with the sarong that still kept him trapped on the bed.

With his free hand and his eyes now able to see it only took him a minute.

"AMY? You still in there?" He leapt off the bed and moved cautiously over to the door.

"Shit. What if she's collapsed in there or something?" he said, more under his breath.

He banged on the door hard. "Amy, can you hear me? Are you okay?" No reply.

He tried the handle expecting it to jar as he pressed down on it with force and was stunned to find it gave way easily. His hand slipped and his momentum nearly sending him tumbling to the floor.

He quickly regained his balance, grasped the handle again and opened the door, bracing himself for what he might find inside.

More nothing. Aside from the tap running there was no sign of Amy, or that she'd ever even been in there.

He yanked back the shower curtain, clutching now at any possible explanation or possibility.

But she wasn't there either.

Billy returned to the bedroom, sat at the foot of the bed in his boxers, and stared in to space.

What the hell's going on? he thought, vaguely contemplating the possibility he'd imagined the whole thing.

He snatched up his phone and pressed a button bringing it to life. Amy's provocative picture appeared, and the look in her eyes as she stared back at Billy felt even more unnerving.

Next, he thought to wake Jake. He could have called Amy, or Issy, or gone straight to their room, but he was panicking and freaking out and needed a friend.

* * *

Jake hadn't gotten a lot of sleep since he'd left Billy's apartment.

He also felt wired and knew that he needed to sober up a bit before he'd be able to get his head down.

He'd raided the apartment fridge, which was full of drinks and snacks. The price list was over by the TV, but he was so in need of anything that could make him stop feeling like this that he didn't even bother to glance at it. He just dove straight in taking anything that looked vaguely appealing.

At first, he'd flicked through all the TV stations, watching a few comedy re-runs, then turned it off after failing to get in to two different films. He couldn't concentrate on anything.

Eventually, he'd gotten up out of bed to check on the storm out of his window.

He could see the wind wasn't as violent as before because the trees were only swaying rather than bending over so far they looked like the bark would either snap or they'd come flying out of the ground, which is how they'd looked earlier when they were all in Billy's apartment.

It was still raining, with a little less force than earlier, but it was still relentless.

Jake was about to return to his bed and give sleep another try, when the sky lit up with lightning.

It was so bright it made him squint and even when he closed his eyes he could still see the vivid jagged slash of light cutting across the dark sky.

He looked down to the beach and along to the pier. Another bolt of lightning illuminated the sky.

And that's when he saw her.

He had to do a double, and then triple take to make sure he wasn't seeing things. But by chance he'd been looking at her on the beach, he just hadn't known it.

Even with the lightning gone, he followed her dark figure scurrying along the sand.

Soaked to the skin, still wearing her green dress, which was now stuck to her body, and half-walking half-running towards the little pier, was Amy.

Another bolt of lightning. It was like someone was intermittently shining a spotlight on her, as if she was escaping from prison and being hunted down by the guards.

Except no one was chasing her, as far as he could tell, and he'd looked all along the beach behind her when the last lightning had struck.

She got to the pier, put her bag on the ground in a relatively dry patch, and bent over to rummage inside.

The lightning seemed to be crackling every couple of minutes now, giving Jake an even better view.

"That doesn't look like someone who is fleeing something. What the hell is she doing?" he asked out loud, paralysed by curiosity and unsure what he should be doing.

And then she was gone, disappearing underneath the pier and heading further up the beach.

"What the—"

There was a knock at the door so loud, Jake physically jumped away from the window.

"Who is it?" he asked, trying to pull himself together.

"It's Billy. Ppen up, please. I need your help!"

Jake's mind was spinning. Billy turning up at his door suddenly sounding fraught and Amy's bizarre beach walk had to be connected.

"Hey," Billy stated when Jake opened the door, unsure how to go on.

Billy was a mess. His dark hair was matted to his head, his eyes were wild, and he was in black shorts and a pale blue t-shirt already sticking to his skin.

"Amy's gone!" he blurted.

Jake had a million questions and plenty to say himself, but he bit his tongue a moment longer, hoping his friend would elaborate and some of this would start to make sense.

Billy took a breath. "She sent me a picture about an hour ago, of her practically naked in her bathroom mirror, and asked if she could come to my apartment. I said yes but when she arrived she was acting, I dunno, wild, and not in a good way."

Jake walked over to the bathroom, grabbed a towel for Billy and walked back over, handing it to him. Billy held it in his hand as he continued with his story.

"She tied me to the bed, blind-folded me with a sleeping mask then said she was going to the bathroom, and would be right back, except she never came back."

Jake turned to look out the window, then back at Billy. Definite weirdness going on.

"I heard the tap running and she put music on, so I assumed she was in there, but eventually I freaked out, got myself loose and she was gone." He started rubbing the towel over his head, his face, then down his arms.

Jake looked at his friend. "I just saw her."

Billy's head popped up, mouth dropped open. "What!? Where?"

"I couldn't sleep so I was at the window checking on the storm. The lightning lit up the beach and that's when I saw her."

Billy started walking towards the window.

Jack continued. "She wasn't exactly running but she was walking very quickly and looked like she was in a hurry. She stopped at the pier," he pointed in its general direction. "Checked something in her bag and then carried on up the beach until I couldn't see her anymore."

Billy peered out into the darkness.

"I don't get it. Why would she leave you tied to the bed then run off down the beach?" Jake asked.

"You said she checked something in her bag?" Billy asked, his voice sounding a bit shrill, despite his best efforts to stay calm.

"Yeh, it looked like she was rummaging around in there, but she didn't pull anything out. She must have just been checking–

"Oh, shit…" Billy exhaled, loudly.

Jake and Billy had the same thought almost at the same moment.

"Come on, let's go. I didn't think for a second to check my backpack but I'm guessing now we're going to find the fucking thing is empty!"

Jake gathered the same white shirt and denim shorts he'd been wearing all evening on the back of a chair and quickly threw them on. He hopped into his trainers and followed Billy quickly out of the door.

They ran the short distance between apartments, bursting through the door, breathless, and headed straight for the backpack.

"Empty. Fuck." Billy threw the backpack on the floor and stood dumbstruck.

"I knew there was something up with her, even in the picture she didn't look right," he said, grabbing his phone and getting the image up on screen to show Jake.

"Wow. I can see why you said yes. Fuck."

"Why the hell would she do this?"

"No idea. She was definitely off key when we first met her on the plane, but I thought she'd chilled out since then."

"I'd never have thought she'd bloody rob us," replied Jake. "What do we do now?"

"We go after her, but we're going to see Issy first.

"Maybe she knows something, and if she doesn't, we have to tell her," Billy stated.

"You're right. She's either in on it—which I just can't believe—or she'll be worried sick when we tell her where Amy's gone."

"Where *has* Amy gone, though?" Billy wondered out loud. They hadn't even thought about her end game until now.

"Oh, no." Billy said, looking over to his bedside table, noticing the keys to the boat were gone.

"We need to hurry. I don't know what the fuck she's doing, aside from trying to kill herself. She's gone for the boat and I'm guessing she's not going to wait until it's light to take it out."

"How does she even know where it is?" Jake asked, exasperated.

"Fuck knows. I guess there can't be that many docks near where we are, and she's made an educated guess. She was going the right way from what you said."

"If she gets to it first, which it looks like she's going to, how are we going to go after her?"

"I've been thinking about that. They have jet-skis here, we're going to have to just take one."

"I've seen the hut where you can hire them down by the beach. The keys are probably hanging in there, we just need to get in," he said.

"You mean we break in, take the keys, and steal a jet-ski!? Are you fucking nuts?"

"Do you have a better idea?" Billy stopped and asked Jake seriously.

Jake's mouth dropped open to speak but no sound came out.

"Me, neither," said Billy. "With a bit of luck, we can return them without anyone being the wiser. Worst case. We abandon them nearby, so they're found quickly in one piece and not much fuss is made. This place isn't really buzzing with police."

"Yeh, I guess."

"It's that or we just sit back and wait to find out if Amy either drowns at sea or finds the first clue and books herself a one-way ticket to Antigua, taking our maps with her and leaving us completely fucked. The next we hear of it will be when we're watching the news one day and that same psychotic hot girl from

Sydney pops up, having discovered a trillion dollars' worth of gold and rare fucking jewels!" Billy spat out, going red in the face.

Jake was taken aback but he knew his friend was suffering even more than he was.

"I'm sorry, man. I feel fucking terrible. This is my fault. If I'd been thinking straight, I wouldn't have fallen for such a stupid trick. I feel like such an idiot," Billy said, shaking.

While they'd been talking, they had made their way to Issy and Amy's room and were now at the door.

"Mate, this is in no way your fault. Amy is the one to blame. I don't know what got in to her, or maybe she's always like this and the other stuff was just an act, it's not like we've known her for ages," Jake said.

The door to the apartment flew open and Issy stood in the doorway wearing grey sleeping shorts and a white top. "What the fuck is going on? And what are you saying about Amy? she demanded. "Where is she!?"

The expression on her face told both boys that Issy was undoubtedly not in on the deceit, there was, to their minds, no way she could be faking.

Jake put his hand on her shoulder. "Amy's… stolen the bottles, and our boat, and we think she's on her way now to try and find the first clue," Jake said, unbelieving his own words as they rolled out of his mouth, along with a clap of thunder overhead.

"That's ridiculous. Why on earth would she do that without me?" Amy sighed. "She's just not herself at the moment but she's not a thief. Amy's got a heart of gold. What happened to her really shook her up and she's been acting tough and impulsive ever since. But I know her, she's my best friend and there is no way she would do something like this. Never."

She looked between both guys. "How do you suppose she got in your apartment undetected and got away without you noticing? And how do you know she's in a boat!?" Issy exclaimed, getting hysterical.

Jake started telling the story and Billy got his phone out and showed Issy the picture to prove they weren't making it up.

"I remember she was strange before I fell asleep. She was just sitting upright on her bed, staring. She said she couldn't sleep, and I told her it was just the rum and… then I fell asleep. She looked distant, and I don't know, her expression was weird. It's the same expression in the photo," Issy said, appearing to reluctantly accept Jake and Billy's account of what was going on.

They told her the rest of the story. Jake explaining how he'd seen her look in her bag before making off up the beach, and their plan to steal a jet-ski.

"We wanted to come and tell you what was going on. We didn't want you to wake up and find everyone gone," Jake said.

"I'm coming with you," Issy said, dashing back inside, looking for her socks and running shoes.

"But, that means we'll need to take two jet-skis," Billy half-protested.

"And?" Issy said defiantly.

"You take one, and me and Issy will go on the other," Jake said.

"I can ride a jet-ski, idiots. Let's go." She shut and locked the door behind her, setting off at a fast jog, leaving Jake and Billy struggling to keep up.

* * *

By the time they arrived at the beach hut, Jake was out of breath and sweating, and Billy could barely stand up.

Issy looked at them both, having hardly raised her heart rate. "Pathetic," she said. "Now, how do we get in here?"

"I…" Billy was struggling to talk. "I think we should kick the door in, if we can. Cause a bit of damage."

Issy and Jake stared at him.

"Real subtle. They'll never know we were here," Issy blurted sarcastically.

"Hear me out. If we make it look like some drunk rampage, it could be anyone, but if we manage to get the lock off it looks more professional, you know? It's going to raise suspicion and require further investigation. That, and do either of you have any clue how to pick a padlock or happen to be carrying around a pair of bolt-cutters?"

The stared back at him, in silence.

"No? Didn't think so," Billy said impatiently, taking a step back and bracing himself.

Jake and Issy stood back, seeing what he was about to do.

Billy kicked the wooden door with his big size eleven shoes, hard, reminding him of when he'd kicked their way out of the tunnel back in Bristol. His leg seemed to bounce off but not before they all heard a loud cracking noise.

The door remained largely intact and the padlock was still attached but enough had given away to convince them it wouldn't take many more kicks to succeed.

"Issy keep watch down that way, and Jake you go keep an eye out up the beach. The hotel might have security checking the beaches at night. If you see anyone, yell an alarm so I know, then run," Billy said, lining himself up again.

Jake walked slowly up the beach, leaving his friend to it for now. Ever since the fight in the cellar, nothing had been normal. He wasn't even surprised he was an accomplice in a jet-ski robbery.

He'd walked about five metres; sixteen feet, when he heard another crack. Billy must have had another go. He turned around and saw his friend limping back to his starting point, obviously unsuccessful.

Another five metres; sixteen feet, and it was getting even darker around him as he got further away from the lights of the resort.

Jake realised at this point he was standing exactly where he'd first spotted Amy in the glare of the lightning. He looked around his feet, half-hoping to find a clue or cry for help or something Amy had dropped, to explain her behaviour.

The only motive they had at the moment was greed, and that she wanted to get hold of the treasure. But, they all also found that hard to believe.

Jake heard another crack behind him, this one more pronounced and successful sounding. It was followed by a much quicker follow-up attempt and a noise that signalled unmistakable success. He had a quick look around, making sure no one was coming, then ran back to the hut.

"Nice one, mate," he said to Billy, seeing the door and the padlock had parted ways. The door now swung open.

Issy arrived at the scene a moment later. "Yes!" she whisper-yelled.

Billy and Issy went inside while Jake remained outside as lookout. "Got them," he heard Billy say.

He walked back to the entrance with a handful of keys. "They were hanging on the back-wall as we'd thought. They've even got numbers on so we shouldn't have any problems. I grabbed a load just in case one doesn't start. Now we just need to find where the jet-skis are kept, shouldn't be too hard."

They walked down to the sea and looked along the beach. Nothing.

Then Issy shouted, "Look. They're up there! I don't know how we missed them."

To the right of the hut as they were facing it with their backs now to the sea, Issy had spotted six trailers made for transporting the jet-skis around.

They were pulled back against the trees, out of view, unless looking for them.

"Let's find the keys that match, test them to make sure they've got petrol, and get them down to the sea."

They checked the numbers on the jet-skis then went through the keys together to find the matching sets.

"Okay. Give it a quick start but only for a few seconds, check the fuel then turn it off."

Issy went first. "Half a tank in this one."

"Full tank in mine," Jake said, going next.

"And mine," said Billy. "Right. Let's drag these two down to the water. If we do one at a time, with all three of us, it should be fine."

After almost half an hour they had manage to get two of the machines in the sea.

Issy was straddling one, holding the handlebars after insisting she drive, and Jake behind her with his arms around her waist.

Billy was on the other.

"We'll carefully follow the coast around and hope that we see her. I think I can find the bay we got to the other day, so Issy, you and Jake follow me. Don't go too fast, the waves aren't huge at the moment, but this storm doesn't feel like it's done yet," he said, starting his engine.

Issy did the same. After a quick glance over his shoulder to make sure they were behind him, Billy set off.

CHAPTER 21: COMPANY

Amy kept blocking out the gnawing feeling that she was doing something wrong and focused instead on her goal.

She must be close now, she could feel it. She slowed the boat down, so it coasted its way up the coast, and the engine was reduced to a low rumble.

Where is it? she thought.

Amy had studied the Barbados map quickly under shelter before she'd set off down the beach in search of the boat.

She had found the compass symbol almost immediately and tried to memorise any big landmarks or jagged bits of coast that would help her know when she'd arrived.

There had been two particularly pointy outcrops of land just before the compass marking on the map with a bay in between, and that's what she was searching for now. She sped up a notch impatiently.

"There it is!" she said to herself triumphantly, spotting the first rocky pier-like formation by the moonlight just in time to swerve further out to sea and avoid hitting it.

She slowed the boat right down again in order to manoeuvre herself clear, before steering back in to the coastline. Just as she was turning the boat jolted hard, and she nearly fell overboard.

She held on to one side for support, as the boat rocked up and down with the waves, and gingerly climbed to her knees.

I didn't hit anything, she thought to herself, looking over the side in the water.

She couldn't make anything out but waves and water in the dim moonlight.

She was about to hit the power again when another thud jolted the boat, this time in the opposite direction.

Amy just managed to stay on her feet this time, bending her knees, and gripping the steering wheel.

"Fuck, fuck, fuck. Easy does it, Amy," she mumbled, trying to stay calm.

She was grateful the waves weren't bigger, and that she was facing the right way now to head out to sea away from these rocks.

Very slowly she nudged the boat deeper in to the blackness and further from shore.

After five or more minutes, and no further bumps, she told herself she must be safe enough to turn and angle the boat back towards land. She just needed to keep half an eye on the rocky outcrop to avoid any further hairy moments.

Seemingly past the worst of it, she set the boat to a moderate speed and returned her gaze in the direction she guessed her prize must be.

Something inside her told her she was so close. She knew if she could just find a place to moor the boat, a bay or beach to get to shore, she'd be able to find a way to the compass. She just knew.

The more she concentrated on the compass, the more her eyes seemed to become accustomed to the night. She could make out almost every detail, and she even saw a few potential beaches she could stop at, but knew they weren't the right one.

Her body tingled from the sea spray and she could feel her senses heighten as she drew nearer. For a second, the clouds parted and a slither of unfiltered moonlight broke free and shone brightly on the water and coast directly in front of her—revealing an almost hidden bay.

If she'd been going faster, or not been as focused and ready to take advantage of the moonlight, she'd have never seen it.

Amy reached for the power, but a huge wave caused her boat to stop almost dead in its tracks. She grasped futilely at thin air as she was knocked backward.

Surely, there aren't more rocks, she thought to herself, immediately dismissing the thought and reaching for the controls again.

THUD. The boat tipped hard to the right as it hit something solid—or did something solid hit the boat?

Amy shut the power off and looked over the side, making sure to stay in the centre this time, daring not to lean over too far.

Nothing.

The sea was calm, the rain had stopped, and the air was still. Even the lightning had ceased terrorising the sky and the clouds had thinned enough to allow more light to escape across the water's surface.

She looked again at the waves lapping gently at her now still boat. "Maybe I imagined it. You did imagine it. Stop being such a freak," she chastised herself out loud, trying to anger herself to scare away the fear.

That's when she saw it.

The tip of a dorsal fin submerging beneath the water not more than a metre; three feet, from the boat.

Amy felt a bead of sweat form at the base of her neck, and drip down her spine, all the way to her tailbone as her body was rapidly overcome with fear.

Then another, and another. She started shaking, and sat in the middle of the boat, almost holding her breath.

The intensity and possessed sense of determination to find the compass evaporated as quickly as it had taken hold of her. Her giant black pupils that had been filled with so much purpose, were now small and only had room for terror.

"They weren't rocks, they weren't fucking rocks," Amy shrieked, thinking back to her earlier collisions.

For what felt like an eternity she sat cross-legged in the middle of the little boat, keeping dead still and silent, hoping the shark would get bored and let her be.

Eventually she dared to put her head up and peeked over both sides and then the back of the boat.

The water was calm, and the moonlight was so bright she had no trouble seeing.

The shore was roughly five metres; sixteen feet, away, and the bay still in view.

It's so close. Just get me on land, she thought.

She stared hard to see if she could map out the best, and quickest, route. And that's when she saw it again.

Directly in her line of vision, the head of the shark breached the surface of the water, its dead eyes staring right at her. It writhed half in and half out of the water, revealing its mid-section, splashing its great tail down on the water as it submerged again.

It was hard to tell its exact size as it contorted its head and body so much, but

Amy guessed it must have been three metres; ten feet, long, at the very least. It was almost as big as the boat.

She screamed and dropped to the bottom of the boat.

She told the parts of her brain that were telling her the shark had been looking at her to shut the fuck up, but still commanded her limbs to collapse so they, and the rest of her body, wouldn't be seen.

"It's not going to let me get to shore. It's going to try and sink me…" Tears of pure dread streamed down her cheeks.

* * *

Jake hung on to Issy tight.

He didn't know if it was because she'd done this a million times before, trusted her own ability and naturally had no fear, or if it was because she was desperately worried about her friend and wanted to catch up with her as quickly as possible, but Issy was forcing the jet-ski to tear across the sea like a demon.

Billy, who was supposed to be leading, struggled to keep up. Had Issy not had to keep slowing down to check she was on the right track with Billy, she would have left him for dust.

Somehow all of them knew she was in grave danger and needed rescuing.

* * *

Amy shuffled closer to the controls across the bottom of the boat.

She knew what she was doing didn't make a lot of sense. The shark couldn't see her through the boat, could it?

But she stayed down and out of sight, nonetheless.

"Maybe it can sense the vibrations and knows exactly where I am," she said shakily.

Amy imagined the hideous, dead eyes looking up at the bottom of the boat from way down in the darkness.

In her mind, the shark carved out a large circular route directly below her and used its powerful tail to gather speed.

The circle the shark was swimming became smaller, and the distance to complete it shorter. The shark seemed to fill with rage and frustration, finally propelling itself out of the spin and upwards, charging towards the shallow inches of wood that separated the water from Amy's bare flesh with its teeth bared.

Amy let out a piercing, high-pitched scream as she imagined in great detail what came next. She immediately slapped a hand over her mouth, regretting what she'd done and tried to calm herself.

Suddenly, she flew through the air and slammed in to the side of the boat, cracking her head against the wood.

The shark had ploughed itself into the right side of the boat, launching her into the left panelling, and dousing her in frothing sea water.

She retained consciousness, just, but felt a sharp pain coming from her temple. Amy reached up to touch the area and winced, recoiling further when she pulled her hand back to find it covered in blood.

Drops were falling onto her dress and the floor of the boat. She heard the shark breach once more nearby, thrashing on the surface of the water as if it could sense the kill was near.

Amy tried to rip off a section of her dress but was too dizzy and weak, so she took her dress off altogether and tied it around her wound to stem the bleeding.

She daren't try to start the engine again. She wedged herself against the driver's seat and resigned herself to wait. Either this thing would get bored of toying with her and swim off, or it would find a way to tip her into the water.

Amy sobbed softly and waited to find out her fate.

* * *

On the horizon, Issy could see the sun creeping up. It was becoming an orange, red, and purple battlefield between storm clouds and rays of sunshine. She couldn't help but think fleetingly how beautiful it was.

"As soon as the sun is out, it's over," she whispered to herself, not fully understanding where the words were coming from but knowing them to be true.

"Fuck this. Hang on, Jake," she yelled over the noise of the jet-ski engine.

Before he had time to protest or question what she was doing, she had twisted the throttle and was giving it everything the jet-ski had. They shot across the water leaving Billy yelling behind them, crashing through wave after wave. Jake had to cling to her tightly just to stay in his seat and not get tossed in the sea.

Jake had no idea how she'd sensed it, but he recognized the smaller of the two craggy outcrops they'd discovered earlier, growing in size in front of them as they quickly approached and knew the spot they were looking for was nearby.

They powered by, Issy leaving mere centimetres; inches, between them and the rocks, rounding the point and straightening up alongside the coast again.

"There!" Issy screamed, tensing her body, and homing in on her target.

Jake looked up ahead and saw the boat. Something was wrong, it wasn't moving and was facing out to sea.

Why didn't she go to shore? he wondered.

Barely had the thought left his mind when the water near the boat fizzed and shot in the air, followed by a dark, bloated object driving it ever upward like a volcano erupting.

As the froth dispersed they saw the enormous striped body of the shark, its mouth gaping wide. One of its jet-black dead eyes fixated on them as the other side of its giant head slammed down hard in to the side of the boat.

Issy was so shocked her arms almost lost control of the steering.

They wobbled and held on, lucky enough not to catch a wave in the front or side, which would surely have sent them into the water with the monster they still couldn't believe they'd just seen.

Issy slowed the jet-ski right down and looked behind her to make sure Billy was still with them. He was closer than they thought and pulled up alongside.

"Did you see that!?" his voice was shaking. "That's a fucking tiger. There aren't supposed to be any sharks here!"

"She's still alive," Issy said, recovering some of her steel.

"That thing wouldn't be attacking an empty boat, we've got to help her."

Issy was about to go when Billy reached across and tried to put his arm on her shoulder. "Wait! We need a plan. If we take a hit like that boat did then we're in the drink with that thing."

"So, what the fuck do we do!?" Issy screamed.

They all looked nervously at the water, which was eerily calm again as though nothing had happened.

"It could be fucking circling us from below right now for all we know!"

"You're right," Billy agreed and shivered. "Let's do this. You go around the front and I'll go close to the shore and try to get to the boat from behind. We're safer on the move, but we still need a plan. Yell if you come up with anything, and let's think fast!"

He opened up the throttle and sped towards the boat, praying he didn't hit a rock, or get hit by the grotesque fish he now knew was lurking somewhere beneath them.

As he shot off across the waves, he heard Issy doing the same a short distance away.

He looked to check on her course and saw no sign of anything following her. Happy as he could be that she was okay, for now, his thoughts returned to his own safety. "If it's not following them..." he mumbled.

Billy looked over his shoulder and the site of the dorsal fin cutting through the surface like an arrow head and gathering speed made him almost come off. His hands clung on and on reflex his wrist gave more throttle.

Despite his boost of speed the shark had closed the gap. Billy glanced over his shoulder just in time to see the snout, dead eyes, and mouth full of jagged teeth lunge for the rear of the jet-ski, clipping the back end and sending him into a spin. The tiger shark, unable to halt its weighty momentum, careened past.

Billy was so full of adrenaline and fear his actions were almost outside his consciousness. He got his jet-ski moving again, and this time he actually hoped he was being followed.

He had a plan, not a good one, but his brain had figured the odds were marginally better than jumping in and making a swim for it. It was all he had.

Billy turned the handlebars and leaned unwillingly close to the water to change his course, so he was heading straight out to sea. He looked over to the boat, hoping to catch sight of Issy and Jake but the spray and the boat blocked his vision.

They're either on the other side, or they've been sunk, he thought, his brain feeding him emotionless information on autopilot. He could care later, if he survived.

He tried to yell and found that his voice was strangled by fear.

Billy hoped Issy was doing what he expected her to do. He had no way of communicating his plan, and if she wasn't he was definitely dead.

They probably all were.

He turned the handlebars and leaned again close to the water feeling sick to his stomach as he did it and daring not to look to his right where his knee was inches from getting wet.

Still no sign of the shark since it last attacked.

As Billy got closer to the boat, his heart leapt to see Issy jumping from her jet-ski and landing inside, where hopefully, Amy was.

Jake was holding on to the side to steady them, even from where Billy was, he could see Jake was shaking.

Before Billy had time to think about anything else, his jet-ski shot in to the air. The shark had powered its heavy body upwards, smacking the bottom of the machine from underneath, trying to flip him upside down.

Fortunately for Billy, his machine didn't land on top of him, unfortunately for him he was knocked clean off and splashed gently in to the sea around a metre; three feet, from where the jet-ski now floated.

Wide-eyed with terror and unable to feel his limbs, he panic-swam as fast as he could. Through the spray he saw the tail of the shark slap down on the water just beyond the point he was swimming towards.

I'm fucking swimming towards it, he thought, terrified.

In moments, he reached his jet-ski and grabbed hold, pulling his body out of the water as quickly as he could, all the while expecting to feel the shark's jaws close around his legs still flailing in the sea.

Either it had grown bored with Billy and had gone to investigate what Jake and Issy where up to, or it was preparing for another attack.

Billy prayed for a moment of rest from this onslaught. His body was beginning to give in and the fear that had been driving him was starting to win out and cripple him instead.

"Come on man, fuck this!" he chastised himself, knowing he had to act, or it would be too late.

The jet-ski roared to life. Billy spun around and headed straight for the boat, which had successfully turned towards the shore while Billy had been occupying the shark.

"YES! Go! That's it, fucking go!" he screamed.

His triumph at seeing Issy and Jake doing what he needed them to do for his plan to work, namely getting on the boat and making a dash for the beach, while he acted as a distraction, was short-lived.

The shark breached and battered the boat from the side, forcing it off course and leaving a dent and scratches so deep it looked like it had been picked up and mauled by an actual tiger.

Billy steered to the left and arced around to the right, so he was approaching the powerboat from behind.

He wanted the shark to follow him, but just when he needed those dead eyes to be giving him their full attention, they were nowhere to be seen.

He slowed slightly to give the shark a chance to reveal its location, hoping that it wouldn't be right underneath him.

Up ahead, the powerboat finally straightened out again and was chugging and lurching towards the beach once more. The jet-ski Jake and Issy had been on was left in its wake. No one was on board now and Billy hoped that meant the three of them were on the boat, and not in the sea, or worse.

He guessed the lone jet-ski wouldn't be much of a distraction for the tiger shark now. The machine looked lifeless, it would know.

Yet for a moment, it seemed like the powerboat and Billy's jet-ski would be able to coast on to the sand without any problem. "Please be fucking distracted. Go and explore the other jet-ski, asshole, please!" Billy declared loudly.

The sun was now fully up, and the water had calmed. Gentle waves lapped at both vessels as they edged ever closer to the shore, and it looked like there was nothing else around them for miles.

But Billy knew better. He maintained his speed and waited for the impending breach that was surely coming. He thought of his three friends in front of him and cut his engine.

"Come on, you bastard," he screamed hysterically, willing the shark to try and pick him off in the hope they would escape.

For what seemed like forever, he watched the boat nose through the water with still no sign of the shark.

Then it hit him.

Billy's world turned upside down, sky and sea spinning, blurring into one.

He fell on his back in the water, flailing his arms and legs, momentum dragging him down below the surface. He forced open his eyes wide in fear, looking for what was surely coming for him.

Directly ahead he could see the bottom of his jet-ski, which although hit hard, must not have been upended.

He didn't look around, instinctively knowing no good could come of it. Instead, he urged every sinew of muscle to propel himself to the jet-ski. He surfaced next to it and clawed his way back on in one motion, throwing his upper body at the machine and dragging his legs after him, lifting them out of the water as quickly as possible.

He reached for the throttle, barely knowing which way was up but certain he needed to get himself moving. The jet-ski sprang to life as he tried to catch his bearings.

The boat was up ahead of him, now tantalisingly close to the beach. The lone jet-ski was drifting over to his left, now out of the battlefield. And the shark, he spun his head around, was behind him. He saw the tip of its dorsal fin submerge as it located him and prepared for another attack.

This is it, thought Billy, exhausted but pleased he would, at least, get one shot at completing his plan.

He gripped the handlebars hard and hung on tightly, giving it full power. The jet-ski bounced and chopped across the water closing quickly on the boat, which looked to be damaged and struggling.

The shark pursued, making a beeline straight for him.

Billy clung on as hard as he could knowing one slip and it would all be over. He glanced back quickly and saw its enormous mass breaching the surface like a submarine, travelling at an incredible speed.

He was almost upon the boat and gaining rapidly, but the shark was right behind him.

"I'm not going to make it." Then Billy saw his chance.

His jet-ski smashed hard in to the back of the boat, jolting it forward and within a few metres; a few feet, of the beach.

He used all his remaining strength to place a foot on the handlebars of his jet-ski, before jumping as far as he could.

The shark propelled its body out of the water and crashed down on the spot where he'd been sitting, just as Billy grabbed hold of a section of panelling on the boat's rear.

The shark slid forward, scraping past him, causing him to scream in agony as its rough hide ripped through his skin. Bleeding, he pulled himself inside the boat, landing with a slap on the decking, like he'd just fallen out of a fisherman's net.

Judging by the expressions on the faces of the others, his injuries didn't look good.

"Come on, faster!" screamed Jake at Issy, who was behind the wheel.

He looked on in horror at the state of his best friend.

Billy was barely conscious, but his brain registered Amy in a tiny ball in Jake's arms, and he felt a slither of hope. His head thudded against the bottom as he gave in to exhaustion and trauma and the boat hit the sand, throwing all of them, including Issy, to the front.

The shark was still thrashing around angrily at the boat's tail, trying manically to get them afloat again before they made it on to dry land and safety.

But it was over.

Issy and Jake carried Amy and Billy over the front of the boat to the beach. Jake, remembering the bottles, made one last foray to the front of the boat, reached down for the handle of the yellow bag, and hauled it to safety with them.

They crawled up the beach just far enough to make sure they were out of the shark's grasp, before collapsing in the morning sun covered in Billy's blood.

CHAPTER 22: TRAPPED

They allowed themselves a few moments sprawled out on the sand for the fear to subside, just enough for each of them to catch their breath.

Jake, remembering Billy was covered in blood, forced himself up so he could see how bad the injuries were.

There appeared to be two wounds, both on the same side of his body. One cut across the side of his stomach and the other was just above his knee.

The cut above his knee was the more substantial of the two but Jake was thankful to conclude that both looked worse than they actually were.

He took off his white shirt and tried to rip it into two pieces, but he didn't have the strength. Instead, he did as Amy had done, and wrapped the whole thing around Billy's knee.

Amy's bleeding had stopped a while ago and Issy was now helping her friend back in to her dress and attempting to clean the wound on her head with the bottom of her top.

She needed water for the procedure to be more effective but there was zero chance she was going to paddle in the shallows to dampen the material.

After around twenty minutes, the injured had been tended to about as best they could, and already they looked more lively.

No one had said a word since they'd crash-landed.

Issy, who'd fared better than anyone during their traumatic ordeal was first to speak up.

"We can't stay here," she began. "The sun is already getting stronger, we have no water or food, so we have to move. And there's obviously no way we're going back in the sea, so we need to find another way."

No one disagreed. They turned to look at their surroundings and the seemingly impassable rocks directly behind them.

The bay looked even more cut off from the mainland than the last time Billy and Jake had been there.

"How are you feeling?" Issy looked at Billy.

He was a mess. The blood that had sprayed out of him had dried and caked to his clothes and skin, making it look like the shark had literally shaken him in its jaws like a doll. His hair was wild and matted.

"I'm okay," he croaked. "Really, I'll be all right."

Issy knelt down next to her friend.

"Amy, how are you, hun? It's over now." She went to gently touch Amy's cheek, but Amy instinctively pulled away as if she was still in grave danger.

Issy persisted and managed to eventually make eye-contact with her friend.

"It's my fault," she croaked hoarsely, before bursting into tears and sobbing uncontrollably into Issy's neck. "It's all my fault."

"It's not, Amy, this isn't your fault. You didn't put that thing in the sea." She rocked Amy back and forth like a child.

Eventually, Amy stopped sobbing and shaking enough to pull her face away from the safety of Issy and look at the faces of those she felt she'd put in this predicament.

Billy and Jake had shuffled closer. They both wanted to make sure she was okay and also if she was going to offer some sort of explanation for the whole stealing their most-prized possession thing; they wanted to be close enough to hear it.

With the sun now up and the water a safe distance away, everyone's heartrates had dropped a notch and they were ready to listen and let their senses deal with something other than fight or flight.

"I..." Amy started but the words didn't want to come out.

"I don't know what came over me, and I know that sounds lame as fuck, but I really don't. I remember drinking the rum then feeling like... all I could think about was that fucking compass. I was still me, but I wasn't at the same time. I know that doesn't make a lot of sense, but I had this fire inside of me to find it. I didn't even have a plan beyond that, nothing," she said.

Billy, Jake, and Issy looked at each other, then back to Amy. It was pretty evident on her face that she believed what she was telling them.

"I didn't even... I don't even care that much about the stupid treasure or whatever it is, I don't!" she declared.

"I wanted to be in on it, and I thought… I thought that whatever you were up to was probably something no one else knew about because you were so secretive. I guessed maybe something had landed in your lap that perhaps shouldn't have, and you were keeping quiet about it, so you could get whatever benefit there was to be had. Because of that, I felt like it was a bit of a free for all. I convinced myself I had every right to know what you were doing, and when I found out, I was determined to get my share, and no one was going to stop me."

Issy sighed.

"I know that sounds fucking crazy. I know it does. I think I just wanted to distract myself from stuff back home and I overheard you talking and I just…got swept up in everything. But you have to believe me—I never intended to steal anything from you, ever. I'd never do that!"

"I hate to bring this up now while everything is so raw, but you did steal from us… from me. You tied me up for fuck's sake," Billy said bluntly.

Amy looked up at him with her light brown eyes and small pupils, a reminder to Billy of how shockingly different she'd been just a few hours ago.

"I know," she said quietly then started sobbing in a messy heap on the ground.

For a moment no one knew what to say.

"It just wasn't me. I know how I am now, and I'd never do that… but I think back to how I felt, how I was earlier and… I don't know… I felt capable of anything. I was out of control, but I feel in control now. That's the best I can explain it."

"Come here," Issy said to her friend, softly putting her arms around her. "I believe you, and we're safe now. That's the end of it."

Jake knelt down and put his arm on Amy's back. "It's in the past," he said.

Amy looked at him surprised, and grateful. Then they all turned to Billy.

"Fuck, it's all part of the adventure, right? Even you couldn't make something that… out there, up." He broke in to a smile, albeit not totally convincing, but enough to patch over the wounds in the group for the meantime.

"Okay. So, what's happened has happened. We need to find a way back inland, to a road, and to help."

"Has anyone got a phone that's working? Mine's dead. Worst case scenario we could call for help and get helicoptered off here, obviously worst case," Issy said.

"Dead," said Billy, pulling out his phone. "Not sure if it's water-logged or the battery but we're not getting anything from this."

"Mine too. Battery's dead," Jake said, holding his phone up.

"Mine's working and it's got twenty-eight percent left!" Amy said excitedly. "But I've got no signal."

Amy went straight to maps and found the bright dot was still showing them on the beach even without a signal. She could see where they were, and she identified the cliff directly behind them. There was solid rock, then a green area then a town just beyond it.

Unfortunately, the knowledge didn't help them get there.

"Everyone good to carry on?" Issy asked, eager to make some physical progress.

Everyone nodded at Issy, grateful she still seemed full of energy and was taking control. It calmed them and gave them a much-needed boost to get up and go.

Jake picked up Amy's bag with the bottles in and put it over his bare shoulder, marching off to look to the left of the beach.

Issy and Amy, took the back-middle section, and Billy wandered off to the right.

The beach was only about a kilometre; a mile, long, so it wouldn't take them long to scour the whole thing for a path or way out, without having to get back on the boat—which each of them had silently made a pact, by looks alone, that they would rather die climbing the rocks than do that and face another ordeal with the tiger shark.

As he shuffled his feet along the sand and closer to the back of the beach, Jake looked over to his left, at the jagged collection of rocks that looked like they'd fallen off the top of the cliff and landed on the shoreline, smashing and freezing where they lay.

He spun around, steering his gaze from the rocks and back out to sea, and along the water's horizon.

The water was a mix of bright blues and turquoises and the sky was now a brilliant blue with only white and grey clouds scattered around. The storm had passed but the air still felt humid and thick.

He looked down from the horizon, pulling his eyes across the surface of the sea, wondering if the shark was still lurking out there, or if now that there was no disturbance on the surface, it had finally swum off to find food elsewhere.

Finally, his gaze hit the sandy beach they were on, and he allowed himself to spin around further to look along the length of it. Palm trees, a few more rocks, and his friends aside, it was pristine and empty.

To have discovered this place for the first time must have been unreal, especially if they came from dark wet England, he thought.

Forcing himself back to the present, he trudged up a gentle slope and started looking to see if there was any path around to the left as he faced the cliff, or if there was any path going straight up that at least one of them could climb.

He took a closer look at the base of the cliff. The rocks were jagged but sharp, not ideal hand-holds for climbing. They were slippery too.

The sea obviously gets back here when the tide's in, he thought. Great, we're on a fucking deadline too.

He continued to look for hand-holds along the rock face, moving slowly to his left and the edge of the beach. Jake hoped the others were having more luck.

By the time he was almost at the edge of the beach his brain was fizzing trying to think of the beginnings of an alternative plan. From where he was standing there was no way through, and no way up without risking a serious fall—he wasn't even sure they could get that far up in the first place.

But still, he wasn't ready to admit to himself, let alone the others, that it might be time to consider the boat lying in the middle of the beach, damaged, and possibly, their only viable option.

He got as close as he could without putting himself in any danger of getting wet, or of anything being able to jump out and grab him and looked over the collection of stones to see if there was a way through.

"Oh, fuck," he whispered as he spotted it.

Jake could see a very narrow, dark gap in the rock face past the boulders maybe five metres; sixteen feet, from where he was standing, which looked very much like the entrance to a cave. He could clearly see a ledge running along the bottom in to the darkness big enough for them to walk on, but he had no idea what it led to, and if indeed it led to anything at all.

Worse still, to get to the narrowest of cave entrances involved jumping from jagged rock to jagged rock with the sea swirling around them powerfully as the waves pushed water in and sucked it back out with equal force.

"Fuck," Jake said again, really hoping Issy, Amy, or Billy had found a better alternative.

He took another glance at the frothing water and turned away with a shiver, walking with some pace back towards the others to learn of their progress.

Up ahead, still roughly in the middle of the beach at the back he saw Amy and Issy pointing up at something, and a little further on he spotted Billy running to meet them.

They must have found something, he thought, relief washing over him. He managed to break in to a trot and hurried as quickly as he could to join them.

"What is it? Have you found a way out?" he yelled as he got closer.

They turned to look at Jake running towards them and he could see immediately from the look on their faces that he was their last remaining hope, and they could see from the disappointment on his face that he was theirs.

"What is it?" asked Jake.

"It's not much," Issy said. "But it might be something. If we can get to that gap there." She pointed, holding her other hand against her forehead to act as a make-shift sun visor. "Then there's a path up. We could climb out."

Jake looked at where she was pointing. She was right, there was almost a ledge.

His eyes followed the rock up to see where he'd put his hands and feet next if he was up there. Another ledge, a hand-hold, a rock jutting out, his eyes slowly traversed the rock face up to the top. His imagination carrying him over and picturing his body collapsing on a flat, dry, and ultimately safe cliff-top.

The others looked at him expectantly and waited for him to catch up. He hadn't spotted the huge drawback in this plan yet and they desperately wanted him to see it, and also come up with an instant solution.

Jake's eyes floated back down to the ledge Issy had initially pointed to.

He then took a step back as he took in as much of the picture as possible. "How the hell do we get up there?" he asked.

"We have no idea," said Amy, sinking to the ground.

Jake had always been a decent climber since school. He was taken on a school trip where they'd done climbing and abseiling and he'd loved it. His biggest passion was surfing, but he occasionally went climbing with a few friends. He was lean, strong, and importantly had a natural technique of getting as tight up against the wall as possible.

He was certain there must be a way up. Even if he could manage to scale the cliff on his own, then he could get help. It was only mid-morning, and when he'd been here last with Billy it'd been early afternoon, and the tide had still been out—they had time.

Jake strained his eyes searching for a way up, searching, searching for the smallest gap or stray rock poking out that he could use as leverage to get his body up to the ledge.

There were a few half-decent looking candidates, but the problem was there was simply nothing around them and no means to get from one to the other.

"It just can't be done," Jake said flatly, after going over a dozen different routes in his head.

"So what do we do? We can't stay here! We have to do something, or we'll starve," Amy exclaimed.

"Actually, we have to get out of here long before that…" Billy said, his voice trailing off, seeing Jake making a gesture behind Issy telling him to shut up.

Billy had also guessed about the tide, but Amy and possibly Issy hadn't, yet.

"What do you mean!?" Amy begged angrily. "Surely that thing can't come up here, we're safe for now, right?"

Issy had been quiet, thinking about the exchange between Jake and Billy. "The tide," she said. "When is high tide? How far is it going to come in?"

"We were here before around two o'clock, I think, and it was still way out, maybe a bit closer than it is now but still a long way out," said Jake backtracking, and feeling guilty for causing even more panic.

He thought about the cave and dreaded telling them even more.

"We've probably got until around six, or maybe even a bit later," said Billy. "But looking at some of these lower rocks, and the stuff that's washed up this far on the beach, my guess is the water will definitely come up this far."

"Yeh. Think that's about right," agreed Jake. "I might have found another way."

All three of their faces lit up at the prospect of another way out. Climbing a wet, slippery cliff face made of jagged, sharp rocks, or getting back in their battered boat to face what now was, by far, their worst nightmare was not much of a choice.

They were ready to jump on any alternative.

"Look. It's… it's probably easiest if I just show you. But, if we decide to go this way it won't be easy," he said, turning to walk back to where he'd just come from. Issy and Billy followed, with Amy just behind them.

"It's not…" she couldn't even get the words out. "Tell me we don't have to go back in the water?"

CHAPTER 23: THE CAVE

"I'm not coming. I can't!" screamed Amy.

They hadn't even made it close enough to see over to the cave as Jake had done. Even getting a few metres; few feet, from the water again was enough to make Amy physically shake, and the others weren't holding up much better.

"Come on, Amy, let's just have a look. We don't have to do it if we all agree it's impossible, but we're quickly running out of options. Nothing's going to get us from that spot of sand I promise." She squeezed her friend's hand, but Amy wasn't moving. She was white as a sheet and seemed to withdraw back in to the place she'd been in when they'd found her on the boat.

"Amy just sit tight there for a minute and we'll check it out. Billy, Issy, have a look and see what you think. You don't have to go too close to the water to see the cave's entrance, just go up to the edge there and then stand on your tip-toes and lean over a bit, Billy you're probably tall enough as it is, mate, you'll be fine."

Jake led them down to the spot and pointed at where they needed to stand while he stood behind them, Amy sat staring terror-stricken a little way behind him.

"I can see it," said Billy.

"Me too," agreed Issy, in an equally dull tone.

There were no shouts of triumph or relief, but Issy, Billy, and Jake gave each other a knowing look and they all resigned themselves to the fact that this was their best chance to get off the beach, assuming they didn't want to get back in the water.

Issy looked over at Amy, and Jake and Billy followed the direction of her glance.

"We can't leave her here," Issy said fiercely, snapping her head back to face them.

"I know, but how are we going to get her across. I think the quickest way over is to jump across those four rocks. One. Two. Three. Four." Jake counted them out so the others could follow.

"The gaps between the rocks in front of the first two, towards the sea, aren't very big. I mean, there are a lot of rocks there so it's unlikely…" Jake trailed off.

They all knew what he was talking about, and they'd all been thinking about it.

"But the last two… there's not a lot of protection in front of those. You could swim right up to them."

"You mean it could swim right up to them, right?" Issy asked, looking scared.

"Yeh, I do. But the chances that the fucking thing is still around and that it'll somehow spot us jumping across these rocks has to be one in a million, but when we get to those last two rocks, yeh, I reckon it could get at us if it really wanted to," Jake said, staring at rocks three and four.

Issy and Billy did the same.

"If we were quick…" Issy thought out loud.

"Yeh, we'd need to be quick, but make sure. You know? We'd have to nail every jump," said Billy.

They stared at the wet stepping-stones covered in froth and spray.

"We don't have a choice," said Jake.

"You're sure there's no way we can climb that rock face?" Issy asked, desperately hoping for an answer different to the truth she already knew.

"There's just no way to reach it, and even if we did, the next hand and foot-holds are just too far apart.

"There's no way we're getting back in that boat, this is our best and only real option.

"If those rocks weren't surrounded by water, I reckon none of us would think twice about hopping across," he said half-heartedly.

The jumps themselves weren't too bad. They were achievable for everyone in their party, but they were still jumps of nearly a metre; two feet, that would need to be executed perfectly.

If they didn't land fully on each stepping stone, they'd slip and fall between them.

They had no idea how strong the waves were or the current below, but the fear was the pushing and pulling motion would either batter them against the narrow cave walls as a surge of water rushed in—or they'd be sucked out into the open sea when it went back out again.

They walked over to where Amy was sitting, still white as a ghost. She knew straight away what the verdict was.

"I can't," she said seriously.

"Look none of us wants to do this but think of the alternative. We sit on this beach watching the tide slowly edge its way up the beach, bringing that fucking hideous thing with it, until eventually we have nowhere left to go."

"Worse still, it'll probably be getting dark," Jake interjected.

"All that thing's got to do is be patient, we have to move," Billy said sternly.

Amy rocked back and forth on the sand. She stood up abruptly and screamed so hard, her voice eventually gave out, making the others jump back.

She looked at them, her face now a pale, greenish-white. "Okay. Show me."

They took Amy back down to the spot and showed her the rocks she'd need to jump on to reach the cave beyond.

Amy was silent through the entire process, concentrating hard. She'd stopped protesting and appeared to have found an inner resilience and determination to survive.

At least they hoped that's what it was. The alternative was to assume she'd given up and was accepting the fact she would slip from existence altogether.

* * *

"I hope that cave goes somewhere," said Jake.

Issy shot him a look, telling him to shut up. They'd been sitting in a small circle, talking, far enough from the sea that each of them was confident nothing could leap out and drag them in.

Amy had finally accepted the cave had to be worth a shot. They'd only discussed that and the cliff-face—the boat just represented certain death in their minds and none of them would even consider it after what they'd been through.

But even though they were now in agreement it didn't mean any of them were happy about it. In fact, now that Amy was no longer holding them back, it meant Issy, Jake, and Billy had no security blanket. Nothing was stopping them each making their leap of faith right now, and yet they'd all decided to sit and rest for a while before making the attempt one at a time.

"Can I go second?" Amy asked, breaking the silence and everyone's nightmarish thoughts.

None of the others had even thought about the order in which they'd go across until that point, and unable to think of any good reason as to why Amy shouldn't go second, they all nodded in acceptance.

"So, who's going first?" she asked.

"I'll go first," said Issy.

"Jake, any preference," Billy asked him.

"I'll go last, mate, you go after Amy," he said, sensing his friend's trepidation.

Billy was thinking about how close he'd come before to getting caught by those jaws, and instinctively covered his bandaged wounds with his hands.

"Thanks, man," he said, unable to protest.

"Okay. Let's do this. I can't sit around any longer. The tide is already starting to creep in, and I'll be fucked if I'm going to give up that easy." Issy got to her feet, picking up Amy's yellow bag with the bottles in it.

"I can take it," she said, catching the looks of both Billy and Jake, who looked like they wanted to take the bag off her.

Amy, who's single-mindedness had returned now that they were resigned to a set course jumped up after her, followed by Jake, and then Billy, who was still gently checking his makeshift bandage.

They walked over to the water's edge, falling in to line single-file, Issy leading the way, Amy just behind, Jake behind her, and Billy looking like a dead-man walking to his execution bringing up the rear.

No more words were spoken, and a heavy serious silence descended.

All they could hear was the sound of the waves crashing against the rocks. Thankfully the waves didn't look too big nor were they hitting their target particularly hard, but there was still enough spray to cause a fatal slip.

Issy stood in front of the rocks, staring at the nearest rock swinging her arms gently, her knees slightly bent, preparing herself. She looked like a long-jumper about to attempt her final jump of the day, needing a perfect score to stay in the competition.

Her arms swung slightly faster and her knees bent slightly more in time with the motion. The others held their breath, unable to watch but completely fixated at the same time.

One final big swing of her arms back behind her, and on the returning upward swing, she launched herself forward in the air, leading with her right foot.

Amy and Jake didn't take their eyes off Issy while Billy furtively cast his gaze between her athletic tense body and the water, half-expecting to see that great striped monster hurl itself at her, jaws wide open.

Issy's right foot landed with a soft slap on the first stepping-stone, her trail leg and the rest of her body nestling safely down with it shortly afterwards.

Jake punched the air and Billy and Amy hugged, pulling away quickly after making awkward eye-contact.

None of them made a sound though. They didn't know if the shark would be able to hear them. The thought would have seemed ridiculous had they not seen what they'd seen, but because of the terrible memory still very much in the front of their minds, minimising noise was a priority that each of them took deadly seriously.

Issy took a quick look to her left at the rocks immediately next to her, guarding her from the sea. She relaxed a little and looked forward again bracing herself for the next leap.

She went through the same process but with less swing, bending her knees slightly, and rotating her arms back and forth. Again, she bent her knees more during the final backward swing and launched herself once more in the air on the upswing, right foot leading.

This time there was more of a splash as her landing coincided with a wave, but it was nothing too big and her footing remained sure and steady.

Issy looked again to her left at the sea. Unbeknownst to her, Jake, Billy, and Amy were doing the same behind her.

They watched her shiver. Probably trying to block out the images piling in her mind, then she shook her head, and looked forward at the task at hand.

They heard her. "Come on, Iss, you got this." She said, before jumping hard. She'd thrown her routine to the wind this time and just threw herself forward on instinct.

Her landing was impeccable, even with the clunking bag on her back.

Balancing in the spray against the backdrop of the cave with waves crashing all around her, she looked tense but strong. Her lean figure standing tall and straight and her honed muscles taught and ready.

Issy looked across to the last rock she needed to reach, before she'd easily be able to hop to the ledge at the opening of the cave.

The others were watching from the other side willing her on and holding their breath.

"Come on, Issy, move," urged Jake, finally exhaling after what had seemed like an eternity.

She leapt high in the air from a standing start and almost overshot the final rock, wobbling as her trailing leg collided with her front leg nearly sending her tumbling in to the most exposed section of water.

It looked deep from where Jake stood, and he felt sick watching and waiting for Issy to right herself and not fall in.

Before she'd even fully regained her balance, Issy quickly made the final hop and hugged the wall of the cave's entrance breathing hard.

The waves and water alone found it difficult to breach the entrance to the thin cave entrance.

She was safe.

They watched as she hugged the rock face, slipped off the bag from her shoulders, and flipped her body around completely so she could look back across where she'd just come from.

"Come on, Amy," she mouthed across the expanse of rocks.

* * *

Amy took one quick glance to her left then swiftly looked away again. She made a final attempt to control her shaking limbs. Her hands subconsciously gripping the sides of her green dress, now tattered and filthy—then she was gone.

One. She landed on the first rock wobbling but on it. She didn't wait to steady herself she just went again. Two. Even more wobbling this time, and very nearly overbalanced.

Issy watched open-mouthed and horrified and Jake and Billy did the same from the beach. Three! She'd transitioned her over-lean into the beginning of her next jump and this one she'd landed both feet squarely on the third rock. Before her feet had any time to reposition themselves, she was in the air again, fierce concentration on her face, blocking out everything but the black stone in front of her. FOUR!

Issy opened her arms wide pulling her friend against her body as she made the final little hop on to the ledge.

"You're fucking amazing, AMAZING!" she whispered aggressively and as loudly as she dared in Amy's ear, bear-hugging her tightly and not letting go.

Two over, two to go.

Issy helped Amy carefully spin her body around so they were both facing the two boys. They were embracing before Billy's attempt.

Billy was feeling more confident than he had been after watching Issy's controlled technique and Amy's fearless dash, carry them both across successfully without incident.

He stood looking at the rocks that led to the cave entrance for the hundredth time and weighed up his approach.

Issy's way had been more sure. She'd never been in any real danger of falling in, and she'd really taken her time with each step. But Amy had been exposed for less time on the last two rocks, which offered no protection to the sea in front of them, or what was in it. Her crossing had taken a matter of seconds in its entirety.

He made his mind up and stepped up to the mark.

Just as Issy had done he bent his knees slightly, lined himself up and began to swing his arms back and forth.

One, two… just as he was bending his legs a fraction more and preparing for the final swing to propel himself across to the first rock, he spotted something from the corner of his eye that distracted his momentum so much he completely lost balance. He found himself on one leg practically stumbling in to the shallows nearest to him.

Billy regained his footing, forgot all about which technique he was going to use and took two steps back, his face turning a see-through white.

Just beyond the fourth rock, he'd seen a fin.

He'd only caught the tip of it from the corner of his eye as it submerged beneath a wave, but Billy was absolutely certain of what he'd seen, and it left him needing to vomit.

Amy and Issy were frantically scouring the water to see if they could see what he'd seen. Jake had his hand on his friend's shoulder as he retched on the beach but was looking back behind them.

Nothing.

On the surface the water looked as clear and as beautiful as it had days ago when they landed, their hearts and heads full of hope and holiday.

This was as far from a holiday as any of them could imagine. Billy finished retching up his guts and pulled himself together.

"I saw it, man," he said to Jake, desperate for his friend to believe him.

"I know."

They stood together looking across at Amy and Issy, who stood helplessly, at the unmovable rocks unbothered by the waves that kept slapping the top of them or the froth or spray bursting from beneath, and finally they looked out to sea.

The expanse of water looked harmless, but they knew differently. Whether Billy had seen a fin or not, Jake just knew the shark was nearby.

The thing was possessed and simply would not leave them be until they'd been shredded and minced and floated in bloody bits among the now tranquil water.

"Go quick, now," Jake turned to Billy and told him urgently.

"If it's out there still, it's not going away and it's probably lining itself up. "Just fucking go and I'll be right behind you." His eyes were wild, and they struck fear in to Billy.

"Okay. Fuck it. But let's get a weapon first—just in case.

"I'm not saying it'll do much good but if I get jumped, this time that thing isn't going to get such an easy ride. I owe it some payback." He finished touching his loosely bandaged wounds.

Jake nodded, and they began to scour the beach for anything that might work. A bit of drift wood, a handy-sized rock, something, anything that would make the shark pause and hopefully stop it in its tracks long enough to escape, if they needed to.

After roughly fifteen minutes of looking they both returned to the same spot, Billy armed with a long piece of wood splintered and sharp at one end, about the length of one of his legs.

"Good find, man," Jake stated.

He'd been less successful and had a pocketful of stones, and one particularly nasty looking paperweight with uneven edges clutched in his hand.

"You too," Billy said, staring at Jake's white knuckles as he gripped the stone he'd found in his hand.

"Let's do it."

They positioned themselves like a relay team at the starting spot with Billy in position to leap and Jake just behind him.

Billy took one last glance over his shoulder at his friend, got a reaffirming nod, and turned back around readying himself.

It was time.

Billy ignored what had gone on before and dispensed of any knee-bent arm-swinging techniques. He put his strongest right leg back behind him and bowed his head, half-like in prayer and half-like preparing for a hundred metre; three hundred feet, sprint.

Then he was gone.

Billy shot in to the air and hit the first rock with his right foot, not even letting his left foot settle before he immediately led from the opposite side and flew through the air to rock two, the toes of his left foot desperately reaching.

As he landed with both feet this time, Jake started his own journey. He was also right-footed and despite wanting to force himself to be quick he couldn't help making sure his first jump was risk-free, similar to the way Issy had handled it.

So far, so good. Billy was on rock two and Jake had landed behind on rock one.

But they both knew this part offered the lowest risk. Rocks three and four were where the real danger lay.

Billy didn't hesitate and leapt again, his concentration absolute and subsequent landing perfect. Three huge steps one after the other was his limit, however, and he found himself with his feet together, knees slightly bent, and body firmly planted on the third rock, vulnerable as hell.

Jake just behind him had made it to rock two.

Billy didn't know why he did it, he didn't want to and there was no logical explanation for it, but he froze.

"BILLY JUMP!" Jake screamed at the top of his lungs behind him, seeing his friend crippled by sudden fear.

Billy took a look back at Jake and saw his friend screaming at him, but he couldn't hear the sound. Then he looked to his left and saw the dorsal fin appear directly right at him and was certain the dead eyes and deadly teeth would shortly follow.

Whether it was fear that forced him onwards or common sense or just sheer luck he would never know, but with the monster still a good two metres; seven feet, away, he made the last jump to rock four and staggered forward falling in to Issy and Amy's grateful, and relieved arms.

As they pulled him tightly close, the shark breached the water baring its rows of teeth and dead eyes.

Jake still stood on rock two, paralysed and white.

The tiger bulldozed its way between rocks three and four as far as it could go snarling and thrashing, and finally trying to twist its body back around towards the sea, when it realised there was no way it could get to Billy, Issy, or Amy.

Jake saw his chance and attempted to jump, but his feet were glued to the expanse of rock he was on.

There was no point in keeping quiet now.

"JUMP! NOW!!" The three of them screamed, but Jake was fixated on the teeth, and its massive hulk of a body writhing in frustration.

When it thrashed and turned enough so he could see its dead eyes had acknowledge him, he almost lost his footing right then and there.

Amy sprang to life before anyone could stop her. She hopped and jumped to rock four and let out a piercing scream bellowing his name as hard as she could.

It appeared to have some impact and Jake took his eyes off the shark long enough to see Amy's fragile body precariously balancing in the most vulnerable section of the crossing, her face a picture of pure anguish.

She looked like she was about to attempt to jump back to rock three, which forced his hand. He couldn't let her risk her life all over again.

Jake tried to block out the tidal wave of teeth, foam, and water that was almost upon him and used every ounce of energy he had left to hurtle in to the air, forgetting completely about the landing.

His foot slipped down the side of rock three and his ankle scraped along the hard surface, his knee cracking against the rock as his calf disappeared below the waterline. Amy screamed, Issy behind her now begging her to come back.

The shark was all but righted and Jake was struggling to get his body back on the tiny platform.

He made a call and prayed it was the right one. Diving forward, head first in to a dark pool in front of him, his arms outstretched to minimise any potential impact.

His body looked tiny as it disappeared almost fully beneath the water as the side of the shark's head smacked hard against the rock he'd just been standing on. It writhed like it was in pain and slipped back in to the waves, the momentum from its weight too much for it to stop.

A few moments later, Jake's head bobbed up, and he searched for the shore.

Billy was ready, on his knees, leapt forward, hoping he'd be able to keep his rear on dry land, and reached out to haul Jake in.

Issy had read his intention and fallen on to his calves to stop him toppling over in to the water. Jake grabbed hold of Billy's forearms.

The shark was snapping all around and turning desperately against the pull of the sea, which was trying to drag it back out of the cave's mouth, before it would just as surely lob it back in to the mix again a few moments later.

Jake kicked his legs, Billy pulled, and Issy sat firm. Jake reached the edge of the ledge just as Amy re-landed. All that was left was to haul him to safety.

Billy strained his back, straightened himself with Issy, and Amy now gripping his waist, shoulders, t-shirt, for leverage, and Jake forced his body out of the water. Every moment his legs remained trailing behind him with the shark thrashing around behind him, sending him close to a heart-attack.

As both feet exited the water clean, Amy looked over his shoulder and saw the shark's efforts had been in vain. The tide had been on their side and despite its enormous power, it had missed its chance and had been thrown unceremoniously back to where it had come from.

She watched its head snap in their direction one final time and caught eye-contact with its black stare before its head slapped down on the spray and submerged, its dorsal fin disappearing quickly beneath the surface without a trace.

CHAPTER 24: DARKNESS

Even after the shark had gone, Issy, Jake, Billy, and Amy clung to each other on the ledge at the entrance to the cave.

For the moment, they were safe, and that was all any of them currently cared about. But they couldn't stay where they were forever.

They hadn't slept for more than twenty-four hours. They were hungry, exhausted, and close to the point of collapse.

"We have to keep moving," said Issy, forcing everyone to break from the moment and contemplate the next task at hand.

Jake looked into the gloom of the cave. He couldn't see a lot, but he could see something, which gave him hope. There was light somewhere in the cave's mouth, and he desperately hoped it meant there was a way out ahead.

None of them could contemplate the alternative, that they'd crossed hell to reach a dead end, and might have to go back to that beach. It was unthinkable. There had to be a way through.

Issy moved slowly along the ledge, shuffling deeper in to the mouth of the cave, feeling her way along.

Jake followed next, gratefully wearing his blood-soaked shirt again after Billy insisted he take it to protect his skin from scraping against the rough cave walls.

He made sure he stayed close enough to Issy to reach out and grab her, in case she slipped or needed help.

Amy was next and being the smallest in the group, had few problems sticking close to the wall on the narrow path. Billy came last, his big feet and body causing him problems.

He slipped a couple of times, scraping some loose pebbles in to the water. They plopped loudly as they hit the surface, causing the others to turn in alarm.

"It's okay," Billy said, frustrated his size was making him the weak link in the chain.

There wasn't a lot to hold on to as they shuffled forward, the walls were almost completely smooth. It made for slow going as each footstep, or shuffle, needed to be made tentatively.

Around twenty metres; sixty-five feet, in to the cave the light from the entrance began to fade, but to their delight there was still a dull glow up ahead giving them just enough visibility to keep going—and meaning there was a good chance there was another way out.

They assumed the water was still on their right, but the further they went in, the harder it was to tell what was next to them.

If there was water there, they had no idea how deep it was, and if it wasn't water maybe there was a big drop. The uncertainty meant the going became even slower. No one was in any mood for taking risks, having so narrowly just escaped death.

Jake inched forward, carefully trying to keep Issy's dark outline close in front of him.

They continued for another ten minutes before Jake heard a shout, and then a splash in front of him.

"Issy!" he screamed, darting forward.

It was at that point they discovered the water to their right was not even a metre; three feet, deep.

"You can let go of me now." Issy laughed. Jake's hands still gripping her waist.

Jake looked sheepish but no one could see as the light was too dim. He backed away and waited for her to retake her position.

They pushed ahead, straining their eyes all around them until finally the dull glow began to get brighter.

As visibility improved, they could see the cave was getting wider and opening out. The dark empty space to their right revealed itself to be little more than a large puddle as far as they could see. Where Issy had slipped appeared to be a fair representation of the whole thing.

The light was now so good they could see all the way to the bottom, guessing it couldn't be more than a metre; three feet, deep at any point. Knowing they were definitely in no grave danger of falling, they spread out a bit to further examine where the light was coming from.

As the cave got wider it began to sharply descend, forcing each of them to walk at odd angles, straining their calves.

After heading down for a few minutes, they saw it. The light breaking in was coming from a hole high up in the ceiling, which allowed daylight from outside to stream down upon them. It was an open door back to the mainland, but it was as unclimbable as the cliff face they'd encountered back on the beach.

"For fuck's sake!" Jake shouted as loud as he could from pure frustration. "There's no way we can get up there."

The light streaming down didn't give them a direct route out, but it did help them see.

Amy, Issy, and Billy desperately searched around them for another option, while Jake slumped to his knees his back resting against a rock, momentarily defeated.

"Look! I think we can get down here, it almost looks like steps!" Issy said, pointing. "It is really steep though."

"It is, but we don't have a choice," Billy said, joining her and looking down the narrow, steep descent.

"Come on, Jake. Let's keep moving," Billy shouted behind him.

Issy again led, scrambling along with Amy almost beside her, with Jake and Billy directly behind them.

The low ceiling was jagged with sharp rocks jutting down, forcing them to crawl underneath. After roughly fifteen minutes of scrambling ever further down in to the depths of the island, fear and panic began to set in.

"It's okay!" Amy yelled back, relieved having been on the verge of a panic attack. "It's levelling out here, and there's more light! Maybe it's a way out!"

They picked up the pace and eventually came out in to a square chamber with a small wall of rocks directly in front of them. This one they were able to climb.

"Look. This way." Jake pointed to the best path up.

Carefully finding their next hand-hold or foot-hold they slowly climbed.

"It's getting really bright up here!" Jake quickened his pace as he neared the top, hoping when he poked his head over the summit he'd see a way out.

He reached up and grabbed hold of the highest rock and hauled himself up and over. The sun hit him hard in the face and he had to squint and adjust his eyes to the fierce new brightness around him.

The first thing he saw was the bright shining sea through a hole in the side of the cave as big as a cinema screen—they'd found the window they'd been looking at that first day on the boat.

"We found it, Billy. We fucking found it!" Jake shouted down in the direction of the others.

He turned and helped them each up, then seeing the girls' expressions, he quickly and excitedly recounted their earlier discovery.

They stood for a second enjoying the sun's heat on their faces, while they took in their new surroundings.

Between them and the edge of the cave was a large, deep, clear pool of crystal-green water. They stepped closer to get a better look.

"It looks deep, I can't make out the bottom," Billy said, straining his eyes.

"This place is stunning," Issy said, alternating between staring into the crystal-green water, and admiring the view of the unnaturally bright, blue sea out of the hole in the side of the cave.

"It is, but I hate to burst everyone's bubble, and forgive me if I'm wrong, but I'm still not seeing a way out?" said a dispirited Amy. Her voice sad, small, and croaky from lack of water.

The lagoon and the view had been so distracting they'd totally forgotten to look for a way out. Their bubble burst, they began scanning the interior for an exit that would take them anywhere other than back the way they had come.

Jake and Issy walked carefully around one side of the pool, feeling along the wall for the unlikeliest of hidden passageways.

Billy and Amy did the same thing on the opposite side.

"Anything?" Billy called out over his shoulder, after ten minutes of looking and no breakthrough.

"No, nothing," Jake said flatly, defeated.

"There has to be a fucking way out of here." Amy sat down with force, angry and fed up.

Jake stood at the edge of the water. The surface was so calm and un-spoilt it almost looked like it was solid.

He tried to work out how deep the water was, thinking it could be anywhere between two to five metres; six to sixteen feet, or maybe even a bit more. Because the water was so clear, it was difficult to gauge how big or far away the rocky formations and stones were resting on the bottom.

They were either pretty small, or really far down.

He was just about to go searching for some stones to throw in and hopefully give him a better idea, when something glinted up at him from the bottom of the pool.

"What the… fuck!"

"What is it?" Billy asked. He'd been watching Jake staring in to the water, desperately trying to think of a plan.

Amy and Issy were in front of the massive open cave window with their arms around each other looking out to sea. They were both dead on their feet.

Amy had spotted a bit of coast further up jutting out in to the water and was leaning forward slightly to get a better look.

Issy kept her arms around her waist and held on as if she suspected some hidden force might try to suck her friend clean out of the cave and back to the sea.

They heard Jake's cry and turned to see what was going on. Hope springing up again inside them.

"I saw… something… it's… look! There," Jake said, pointing and animated. "It's… I'm not sure but something is glinting from the bottom of this thing, and it looks like it's made of metal. There's sand or dirt on it so I can't make it out properly, but that's got to be it, right? That's the goddamn compass!"

Billy had been on the same train of thought, but it took Issy and Amy a moment to catch up.

"But, what is it? And how does it help us?" Amy said angrily, overwhelmed by tiredness and frustration.

Jake was close to snapping back at her and wanted to scream. He didn't know how it helped them either and that made him as angry as Amy, but he had to distract himself from their grim situation in order to keep going.

Right now, he needed them to buy in to this.

He just managed to keep his temper in check.

"We're going to get out of this, we will. That tunnel we came through to get here, I'm sure we haven't explored all of it. It was too dark. There's no way out of this chamber but I'm damn sure there's a way out of this cave that doesn't involve climbing back out on to the beach…" He didn't need to offer any more details about what was beyond the beach. They all knew what he was thinking about.

"It's like the tunnel where we found the bottle in the first place. Pirates used to have secret ways of taking shit between their ships and the towns they rocked up at. If that object in there is the first of the two compasses, and it was put there by some pirate years ago, for shit sure he had another way back to the mainland. There will be another way out," Jake finished firmly.

He didn't know if everything he'd said was true, he didn't know that much about pirates or what they did on far flung islands like this one hundreds of years ago. But it made sense to him, and he had to believe. And he needed the others to believe too.

"Right. So, who's going in?" Billy offered up, breaking the tension and showing his support for the plan.

"I'll go," said Jake, already unbuttoning his crumpled, blood-soaked shirt, and kicking off one of his wet, sandy shoes.

He quickly stripped off, and loosely folded his clothes in a pile away from the water so they'd remain dry. Before anyone had any time to really object, he was at the edge of the pool, wearing just black boxer shorts and a determined expression.

Had they been in happier circumstances, Amy most likely would have made some sarcastic joke about Jake in his boxers in front of them, but in these circumstances, she just looked like she wanted to cry.

"Good luck," Issy said. "If it's a lot deeper than it looks, don't panic. Just come back up for air and we can figure out a new plan."

He looked at her, nodded, and slowly lowered his body in to the water, taking a breath as each body part was affronted by the temperature drop before gradually acclimatising.

Once he was in up to his neck he extended his legs, treading water as carefully as he could. He was slightly unnerved to find he couldn't touch the bottom.

"It's lovely once you're in." He smiled weakly, trying to lighten the mood.

Jake counted to three in his head. On three he took a deep breath and submerged, rolling his body in to a gentle dive, head first into the unknown.

He opened his eyes and forced himself to keep them open so he could get used to the sensation and see where he was going.

The pool was big and deep enough that he felt like he had space. He made a wide arc with his arms and kicked his legs once, allowing his body to drift further downward towards the bottom.

As he cut through the water, he cast his eyes across the floor trying to latch on to the same glint he'd seen from the surface.

There you are, he thought, as he spotted his prize.

Another half kick and the object began to take shape. He was less than a metre; three feet, away now. As his face edged nearer, he could see the object that had caught his eye was a piece of metal resting flat on the sandy floor, half-buried.

When Jake reached his mark he turned his head three hundred and sixty degrees, looking for something to grab to steady himself, and what he saw almost made him intake a breath. He caught himself just in time and pinched his nose, trying to calm down. His chest tightened, and his head pounded.

About two, maybe three metres; six, maybe nine feet, away to his left—he could see light.

It wasn't so bright he thought he could just swim up and out and they'd be free, but he had no doubt that the light was coming from the surface. Jake had finally found a tunnel leading out, the only problem was, it was under water.

For a few long seconds he didn't know what to do. To his left lay a possible escape route, and directly below him was probably the thing they'd come to the Caribbean to discover, already nearly dying in the process.

The pressure in his chest was building and he knew even if he wanted to explore the underwater tunnel, he didn't have enough oxygen in his lungs to do it now. He'd have to return to the surface and come back.

And what if it's another dead end? he thought, trying to push that notion from his mind.

Jake turned back to the metal below him and grabbed hold of it with both hands, determined to make some more progress with one of his objectives before his air completely ran out.

It was solid and heavier than he'd expected, and barely budged as he clung on. He pulled the rest of his body closer and started wiping away the sand and dirt and digging around it as best he could to hopefully reveal what it was.

After a few seconds solid work, he'd managed to expose more metal, revealing a flattened pole not even a metre; about ten inches, wide, and about as long as his arm. He wanted to continue but desperately needed air. Resisting a panicked sprint back to the surface, he forced himself to steadily swim towards the light.

"He's here!" Issy shouted.

His first gasp for breath was a desperate one causing him to choke. Billy, Issy, and Amy reached down and wrapped their arms around him so they could drag him out of the water.

"Take your time," Billy said, trying to calm Jake down. He was urgently trying to talk, but still coughing and choking on cave water and gasping for breath.

"Tunnel... there's a tunnel!"

"What? Could you see where it goes? Can we get out that way?" Billy pressed, hope filling his voice.

"How deep is it... how long would we have to hold our breath?" Amy asked.

Jake steadied his breathing as quickly as he could and sat with his arms hugging his knees.

"I'm not sure, but I saw light. It looks like it goes to the surface, somewhere. I ran out of breath so I couldn't go and look properly, but I was really careful on the way down. I took a lot longer than I needed to, then I was looking around for a bit. I won't waste any air next time. It's got to be worth a try."

A short silence followed, each of them looking furtively around for answers. They flitted between excitement at the thought of imminent escape, and fear and dread at the thought of possibly drowning in an underwater tunnel.

"I'm going to go back and check it out. There's no point all of us going until we know more, it might not lead anywhere… but… it might," Jake said, unable to think of anything better to say.

"And it has to be me," Jake added, before Billy had a chance to speak. "I'll be much quicker this time, I know the layout now.

"Can you see the metal thing from up here now?" he asked.

They'd almost forgotten about their treasure with news of the underwater tunnel, and none of them had been able to get a good look while Jake was in the pool because his body blocked their vision.

They jumped over to the water's edged and peered down.

"What is it? It's loads bigger now," Amy said.

You could clearly make out the flat thick piece of metal now, parts uncovered by rust and dirt just enough to catch the light and reflect it back up.

"I think I can dig it out. I was making some good progress but then ran out of air.

"I'm going back in. I'll finish the job with this metal thing first, then I'll come up for air and go back down and explore the tunnel."

Before anyone could disagree with the plan he was in the water taking in as big a lung-full of air as he could manage.

Then he was gone again.

CHAPTER 25: LIGHT

As Jake worked away to fully uncover the metal object he couldn't help but frequently look over to his left at the glowing light.

Please be our way out, he thought, before turning his head back to the task at hand.

He'd managed to uncover the full length of the metal one way, it was like a thick, flat, narrow pole and at the top it had three small points spilling out of it like a tiny metal fountain, with a hollow circle in the middle of it. When he found that part he was certain it was a clue, but he had no idea what it meant.

We have to solve this while we're here because even if we make it out of here, there's no way we're taking this thing with us, he thought.

It was so heavy it would either take two of them, or if they had some rope they could come down, tie the rope around it, head back to the top and heave it out in their own time.

But they didn't have any rope, and they didn't have that much time. They were starving, exhausted, and on the brink. They needed to find whatever clue was to be found and get out while they still had enough energy to do so.

Jake's breath lasted just enough for him to find that there was a lot more metal buried at the other end.

Fuck it, he thought, remembering the other occasions he'd offered up those words already on this adventure, allowing himself a flickering smile.

With his breath short on supply and still what appeared to be a fair bit of work left to completely reveal the metal object and any secrets it was hiding, he decided to see if he could just wrench it free.

Jake grasped the metal pole around the middle, brought his feet either side, planted them on the ground and heaved.

The exertion caused him to see spots, but his efforts were largely successful. While some of the metal remained covered, he had been able to move the whole thing a bit from its original position, giving him a much better visual of the object in its entirety.

He could see there were two curved sections either side of the pole, forming a large arc at the opposite end to the circle with a hole in it.

He suspected what it might be but wanted to make sure before telling the others.

Jake quickly returned to the surface, took a few breaths, and then another massive lung-full before diving down again, without giving anyone an opportunity to speak.

His hands got to work straight away rubbing at the now looser dirt. *It's an anchor!*

There is no way this got here by accident. He grinned under water, excitement surging through his body.

He swam back to the surface to report his find. The others were waiting hungrily for news and he was just as keen to deliver it.

"It's an anchor. There's a loophole at the top where they could tie the rope." He climbed out of the water and collapsed on the side, breathing hard. "It curves at the bottom either side of a sharp point in the middle. It's definitely…" He gasped for air. "An anchor."

They looked down, waiting for the ripples to clear to see what Jake had described.

As the water became calm again their view became less obstructed, and they could see it clearly.

"Did you move it at all when you were digging it out?" Billy looked at Jake. He moved as close as he could to Jake, crowding him in his enthusiasm for the answer.

"I mean, did you change its position at all? Is it still facing the same way?"

"I pulled at it and made it shift a little but it's heavy and completely stuck in the ground. It only became loose and budged a little before I came back up. Why…"

He was about to ask Billy why he wanted to know when the answer came to him.

Jake peered hard down at the anchor and could see it, it looked like an arrow and it was pointing out to sea.

"You think it's pointing us in the direction of the third island?" Jake blurted.

"That's exactly what I think!" Billy exclaimed.

"It does look like it's pointing, now that you've said it. It's pointing out of that hole in the wall and out to sea," agreed Issy. "Anyone got a phone still working? We can screenshot our location on the map and also take pictures of everything and work out exactly what angle it's pointing at when we're out of here. My battery is dead."

"Mine should be good." Amy jumped up. She got her phone from the yellow bag, which Issy had placed carefully by the cave wall. She'd turned it off on the beach to save battery and was happy to see the screen flash to life when she pressed the button.

She still had no signal, but the little dot on the map was still there and it appeared to match up with where they were. She took a screenshot when she found it. She then stood over the edge of the pool taking as many pictures as she could.

At first, she struggled to get great clarity but after trying a few different positions she got a couple of decent shots. She then took pictures of the interior of the cave, the hole in the wall looking out to sea, and the way they had come from, just so they could map all the pieces together and be as accurate as possible when plotting their next course.

Assuming we ever get out, she thought to herself.

She directed and moved the others around where she needed a marker in the picture and made a note of the image she'd taken, standing directly behind the arrow anchor below her in the pool, capturing an image pointing in exactly the same direction the arrow appeared to be pointing.

"I think I've got everything I can get," Amy said. "It's not perfect but we should be able to put all of this together afterwards and draw out a pretty accurate line from where this arrow looks like it's pointing. Can we get the fuck out of here now?"

"Wait. One more thing. Sorry, can I see your phone?" Billy said, something dawning on him. He held out his hand and took the device.

"Yes! Found it, there you go—a compass. It's an app built in to the phone, no one ever uses it, so they don't know it's there, but I found it playing around once and thought it was cool. Stand exactly behind the anchor and point the phone in the same way it's pointing, we should get the exact direction we need. It should also give us our exact location in coordinates. Then take another screenshot—sorted," Billy said, pleased with himself.

"Well remembered, mate. That's genius," said Jake.

Job one complete. All thoughts returned to getting out.

Jake stepped to the edge of the pool once again, looking utterly exhausted.

"Right. I'll try and see how far along the tunnel I can get then I'll report back. Wish me luck," he said, slipping back in to the water.

He swam carefully but quickly down, keeping the anchor to his right and readying himself to head straight to the light.

As he reached the bottom he arched around to the left and kicked his legs once, hard. Jake rapidly approached the gap the light was coming through and was thankful to find the tunnel wasn't too claustrophobic, offering just enough room for him to swim breaststroke.

The further along he got the brighter the light ahead became. He studied the inside walls of the tunnel up ahead to try and spot any sharp outcrops or dangers that would cause him, or the others if he dragged them all down here after him, too many problems.

So far so good, he thought. Trying to keep his pace steady, but not too slow. He still had plenty of air in his lungs, and the going wasn't too uncomfortable, yet.

As the light got brighter and brighter he felt like he was about to emerge from a deep, dark lake. He thought of what the air might taste like when he took his first breath through his mouth, and how tall the trees would be.

He'd always loved the huge pine trees when he'd gone camping with his dad when he was younger. He loved the outdoors and spending time with his dad, just the two of them… Jake relaxed, closed his eyes, and started to drift.

His arm scraped against the tunnel wall shocking him back to consciousness. It took all his focus to stop him taking a deep lungful of water.

The realisation hit him hard that he now didn't have enough air to return back. He'd been so convinced this was the way, and so lured in by the bright light that he'd just gone for it.

Now he found his lungs were burning, his head and eyes were pulsating, and he was so desperate to breathe every second was a battle to stop his body giving in, and just letting the water flood into his nose and mouth.

As the temptation was about to become too strong the underwater tunnel widened out and the light shone at its brightest. Seconds later he crashed through the surface, finally giving into the need to gather air into his lungs.

He tried to vacuum so much air in through his mouth and nose at once that his body didn't function properly, and his attempts actually prevented him from taking in oxygen.

Jake managed to calm down, sensing his survival depended on it and took in the air he desperately needed. Once his breathing was controlled he allowed himself to process how close he'd come to dying for the second time that day.

After a few minutes the oxygen and sunshine soothing him, his eyes took in his new surroundings. All he could see was green.

There were lush plants, leaves, vines, and trees around him in every direction.

He was back on the mainland. And even better, he could see a trail leading further away from the sea and inland—he'd found their way out.

Now he just had to get the others through it without killing them on the way.

CHAPTER 26: JUNGLE

"We can get out!" His words and head bursting through the surface of the pool simultaneously as he returned to the others.

As they helped pull Jake out of the lagoon again, he imparted as much information as he could, getting most excited when he told them about the path he'd seen in to the dense forest, which surely must head inland to civilization.

"How long did it take to get there? You were gone a lot longer than last time," Amy said, sensing there was a 'but' coming.

Jake paused his rapid talking and they looked at him intensely. "It's not… comfortable, but it's okay." He lied.

He'd been torn. Part of him felt obliged to give them full disclosure. They had a right to know what they were getting themselves in to, and if anything went wrong because he hadn't told them what to expect he'd never forgive himself.

But he also knew that if he told them he had very nearly passed out and not made it out of the tunnel at all, there was a big risk they wouldn't get in the water at all, and it would all just end in this cave.

He really couldn't think of another choice, or at least a better choice. Returning to the darkness back towards the sea really didn't feel like much of an option.

"You'll have to hold your breath for a few minutes, so be prepared for that. But as long as you stay calm and keep going then you'll be fine, and once you're through you're out in the open.

"Out of this cave and off the beach," he added, thinking about the green foliage and sounds of the forest, and the path that must lead to freedom.

"Okay. Let's do it," Issy said. "Is there enough room for the bag?"

"Yeh. It's not too narrow, that's the good thing. It's just a bit long. Make sure you swim smooth but steady. I'd be confident doing it again, so I can take the bag," he said, feeling anything but.

He knelt down next to the bag, opened it, collected his shoes and clothes and stuffed them inside.

He then gathered them in a small circle, sitting cross-legged, so they could listen to Jake talk through his experience in as much detail as he could remember.

Issy, Amy, and Billy hung on every word trying to memorise the route perfectly to safeguard themselves against anything going wrong as much as possible.

After Jake's information had been exhausted. They discussed the order and agreed Jake should go first, followed by Amy, then Billy, and Issy last. They decided they would go single-file so as not to make the tunnel a squeeze when it needn't be, but one person should immediately follow after the other with little gap in between.

That way if any of them got in to any kind of trouble, the person behind them would see and could help them out.

In Issy's case, because she was at the back, Billy said he would check every five or ten seconds to make sure she was okay, and in return she would make the 'perfect' symbol with her fingers to tell him to carry on.

Most importantly—and Jake had stressed the point so much in his induction that each of them guessed the journey was nowhere-near as comfortable as he was making out—they needed to be fast. No mistakes.

After giving each other a few hugs and making sure everyone's clothes were fastened tight to reduce drag, they began their final journey.

Jake took one last look at the anxious faces looking down at him before he twisted his body in the water, finding himself less agile than he was with the bag now secured to his body, and dived down for the final time, trying to stay as calm as possible.

Amy knew the stakes, and she knew she couldn't hang around once Jake had gone in the water, they'd discussed that everyone had to follow as quickly as possible.

With this in mind, she forced herself to take an enormous breath, filling her mouth and lungs with air, before twisting and reaching down in to the water in front of her, flipping her legs so they were above her, and swiftly following after Jake.

Without incident they assumed their positions. By the time Issy was fully in at the back, Jake had turned left at the bottom of the pool and was lunging towards the entrance to the underwater tunnel.

Each of them swam carefully but urgently knowing a single mistake would probably cost them everything.

The idea to go head to toe had been a solid one. Amy's only focus was to stick to Jake's heels and let him pull her through. She didn't leave any place in her brain for doubt or fear, just his toes gently moving along in front of her.

Billy was largely doing the same but by midway through the tunnel he began to feel the pressure on his chest and behind his eyes. He was doing his best to block it out and just get through it, but he quietly prayed the tunnel would open out soon.

Issy's only concern was the traffic up ahead of her. She was an excellent swimmer and her lung capacity from all the sport she did was really helping. She looked up ahead feeling no discomfort so far and thought about how happy she'd be to get on dry land and stay on it for a while.

After a minute longer, Jake shot out of the pool on the other side. He'd done the journey much quicker than before, even with the bag, and as soon as he'd dragged himself out over the top onto the soft mud he turned to reach for Amy.

Amy popped her head up and reached up instantly. Jake planted his knees in the ground and strained his body as he pulled Amy clear of the water. She landed on top of him, rolled off, and both of them turned back to the water to look for Billy.

They'd been as efficient as possible through the tunnel and Amy hadn't realised she'd actually left Billy behind.

Billy could see the light ahead, but his vision was becoming blurry, and he swore the light was getting dimmer.

Shouldn't it be getting brighter? Where's Amy? His brain slow to find the words, or the answers inside his own head.

He thought about his parents back in America. Hid dad, almost certainly sitting in his office at his desk.

He might as well move his bed in there. Billy thought to himself. I wonder what mom's doing? Probably something similar. Fucking workaholics.

Billy didn't feel like developing his thoughts on his parents any further.

He felt lazy, and sleepy and decided he'd just rest a bit then carry on later.

Then he felt a sharp pain on his arm that forced him to open his eyes and brought him one step back to reality.

When Issy had realised Billy had slowed right down she had initially thought he was finding his way, or there was a turn up ahead. Her lungs were feeling tighter, but she knew she could hold out a while yet, so she'd patiently waited. Then when she saw Billy wasn't looking for anything, he'd simply stopped moving and was floating perilously up ahead of her, she'd pushed her arms and kicked her legs, darting forward.

She swam up alongside him grateful there was just about enough room for both of them. His eyes were closed so she pinched his arm hard, then quickly covered his mouth and nose not wanting him to breath in.

Billy could barely see, but he was back in the present and knew he was in danger. He felt Issy's pull dragging him along, and her hand around his mouth and nose reminded him not to take in water, even though all he wanted to do was breath in deeply.

He scrabbled his arms along the tunnel floor pushing himself along and helping to maintain their momentum.

Issy saw hands in the water up ahead reaching for them. They were only half a metre; just over a foot, away now.

A final hard kick with her legs and Jake managed to grab hold of Billy's t-shirt.

Amy had her face in the water and could see Billy's deathly pale skin, he looked like a floating corpse. Issy, in contrast looked fiercely determined. She positioned herself beneath his frame and pushed up as hard as she could.

Between Jake and Amy pulling from above, and Issy pushing Billy from below, they managed to get him out of the water and on to his back.

Jake knew CPR and immediately gave Billy mouth to mouth while Amy made sure Issy made it safely out of the water.

Billy coughed and turned, spewing water on the muddy ground.

"Oh, thank fuck," was all Jake could manage, rocking back on his heels, panting hard.

It took Billy a few minutes to get his breath back, but he'd made it, they all had. They lay on the damp earth shattered and bruised—but alive.

"You scared me, you big fuck," Jake said to the air, lying on his back now, alongside Billy.

"I need to give up the cigs man." He tried to laugh but only managed another violent coughing fit, bringing up more of the green lagoon water he'd swallowed.

They lay on the ground a while longer. The four of them in a row like soldiers, looking up at the big palm leaves shading them from the sun's blazing hot rays.

We're safe, Jake thought, closed his eyes and fell asleep.

CHAPTER 27: SANCTUARY

When Jake awoke, at first, he had no idea where he was. Then it came flooding back to him.

Each memory so vivid and shocking he screwed up his eyes to try and make them stop. He couldn't believe they'd been through so much in the last twenty-four hours.

Then he remembered they'd found the compass, and they were out of any immediate danger. Hopefully now near where they could get some food and have a shower.

He had no idea how long they'd slept for, but when he looked over and saw the others still out cold and breathing heavily he knew however long it was, they must have needed it.

He shifted his weight to his left elbow and leveraged himself up on his feet. His body was in bits. Every muscle was aching, weak, and shaky.

Before waking the others he decided to do a bit of a recon, so he could formulate a plan. Then when they did wake up he could hopefully tell them he'd found the way to go, which he hoped would help keep spirits up and get them moving.

He located the trail he'd spotted the first time he was here and went to take a look.

The path was loosely covered with vines and roots but there was no doubt it was there, and Jake suspected they were not the first to make use of it. He imagined their mystery pirate making their way through the undergrowth after securing the anchor exactly where he wanted it in the lagoon down below.

Jake began making his way along the path, pulling back some of the branches, snapping the wood where he could and ignoring it when it was too supple.

After walking a little way up he was surprised at how easy the going was after their previous ordeals. The path was only about half a metre; one foot, wide, so they'd have to go single file again, but the only obstacles appeared to be a few low hanging branches. If they had something to hack away at the strays that would really help but compared to what they'd already been through this would be nothing.

As the trail continued uphill and steepened, he found stones lodged in the mud at big changes in the gradient, which looked very much like steps. The longer he remained walking the more certain he was that he was not the first person to have taken this route.

Deciding he'd gone far enough Jake returned to the others to find Billy stirring, but Amy and Issy were still fast asleep and looked completely out of it.

"I've got to say, man, you've looked better." Billy grinned looking at Jake's blood and dirt covered shirt and his matted hair with tufts sticking out.

"You don't look so hot yourself!" He laughed. He took Billy's arm and helped him to his feet.

"So, tell me some good news. There's a burger joint just past that tree, right?"

"Not that tree, but I'd bet it can't be that far away. I've only been along the path for about ten minutes. We came from that way, so the sea is over there, which means this path takes us in and up. We follow it along and we'll hit civilization in no time. Hopefully this'll take us out right next to some holiday resort or hotel."

"I'm sure they're going to welcome us with open arms," Billy said, looking at the state of his friend again, especially his shirt.

"We'll just say we went trekking and fell down some rocks. We were trapped for ages before finally climbing our way out, explaining why we all look like shit."

Jake didn't really feel like being interrogated about what they'd been through, by anyone. He didn't want to relive the nightmare in the sea, and he definitely didn't want to have to explain what they'd been doing out there in the early hours of the morning.

"Yeh, I don't know how hot the police are over here, but we don't want them putting missing tourists and missing jet-skis together and figuring out it was us."

"There are clean t-shirts in the bag," Amy said as she sat up.

"Sorry, I heard you talking about your shirt and remembered. We can get through this jungle path then try and freshen ourselves up a bit and get changed in to what's in the bag. That way we can just find somewhere to eat and say we've been for a morning swim. My purse is in the bag. I think the cash shouldn't be too wet, but I have cards if not. My phone is in there as well, it's waterproof but I wanted to make sure. We can check the map and see if I have signal too."

Jake sat back down next to the bag and undid the zip. He reached in and found the purse, which was made of plastic and already seemed dry-enough, and gently threw it over to Amy.

The first thing she did was to test the phone. Thankfully, it flashed to life.

"It's working fine and down to twenty percent. No signal still, but the GPS is showing we're out of the cave, and Jake's right, the forest isn't too thick and there's a town on the other side. According to this, it's less than two kilometres; one mile, away, then we should hit a road."

Jake reached back in the bag and found the three wrapped bottles still held snuggly in Billy's t-shirts.

He pulled them out one by one and unwrapped them.

"The t-shirts are damp but clean. We can dry them in the sun for a bit then swap our tops when we hit the road, or wherever this path comes out. Amy there's a turquoise-green scarf in here with yellow pineapples on, I'm assuming it's yours? Your dress doesn't look too bad, incredibly, and if you wrap this around you no one will tell you haven't just been to the beach."

Along with the sarong with a pineapple pattern, there was a bright red t-shirt with a black palm tree leaning over on the chest, a light green t-shirt with a sunset print on it, and a grey t-shirt with a prowling lion on the front.

Jake draped the lion t-shirt over the bag and put the others carefully on patches of ground that were in the sun.

They sat in the shade and waited around ten minutes, looking around for any natural source of water or food.

"We should go. We can keep looking for food and drink on the way but hopefully this walk isn't going to take too long," Jake said, putting the nearly dry t-shirts back around each bottle as neatly as he could, slinging the bag over his shoulder once more.

Then they set off briskly, or as fast as the slowest member of their group could manage, which at this point was Billy.

Billy being the biggest appeared to be suffering the worst from lack of sustenance, and although he was trying his best not to show it—they all could tell. Worried about him, they positioned Billy second in line behind Jake at the front, who'd resumed leadership, with Amy next and Issy happy to go at the back.

She felt extremely protective of Amy and wanted to be first at hand if she needed any help.

For a solid half an hour they wound their way along and up the trail, pushing vines and creepers aside, dodging branches, and forcing their legs to push them up big steps built in to the mud.

Then finally, they saw the end.

"There's a road!" Jake exclaimed, stopping the others.

"We fucking did it," he said, collapsing in a heap around ten metres; thirty feet, from the edge of the forest where they could see the road.

They saw an old, red car rumble past in the distance.

Completely spent and in desperate need of something to drink and then something to eat, the others slumped to the ground too.

"Okay. Let's change our clothes and go and find the nearest restaurant," Jake said, not wanting to stop for too long for fear they wouldn't be able to get back up.

Jake unwrapped each bottle carefully and handed out the t-shirts which felt damp but not too bad.

He gave Issy the green t-shirt with the sunset, Billy the red one with the palm tree, and he handed Amy her sarong, taking the grey t-shirt with the lion on it to replace his ruined white shirt.

After they'd changed their tops, they stood examining each other to make sure they looked respectable.

Billy's visible cut needed cleaning but the majority of spilled blood that had dried on him had been washed away in the lagoon. It still looked bad but unless you were looking for it, it wasn't instantly remarkable. Amy reached up and tried to smooth his hair over to one side, but it just kept springing up again, making her laugh.

Issy looked like she belonged on Huntington Beach, California. She'd untied her hair and had tried to comb it as best she could with her fingers, so it hung loose and long around her shoulders. The green t-shirt really suited her, and because it was a size large, it looked like it was intentionally oversized and fashionable, coming down to her thighs and just covering her shorts.

Amy looked surprisingly fresh too. The sarong hid the rips, dirt, and blood she had on her green dress, and it was impossible to tell she'd been anywhere but the beach. Issy had helped her clean up her head wound when they were in the cave, and now she was styling her hair to cover it as well as possible.

Jake looked tired, but otherwise respectable. His denim shorts had been ripped to begin with and had held up well, and when he'd removed the shirt with the blood, which had been a constant reminder to all of them of the violence they'd endured, he was transformed. The lion t-shirt suited him.

"We scrub up all right, no?" Amy grinned, reading their thoughts. "Come on, let's get some food."

Billy followed behind Jake, trying to keep up as best he could.

When they poked their heads out through the foliage, the bright sunshine no longer obscured by the trees, made them squint.

They could see rows of pastel red, yellow, and green houses in front of them with palm trees dotted in between.

The road was very quiet, and they made it across without seeing a single car.

"Down there. Look," Issy said, pointing to a cluster of buildings that looked bigger than the others and more crowded.

"That doesn't look residential, I bet there's a restaurant there."

With the thought of water, chicken, shrimp, and all kinds of foods running through their minds they hurried their feet along as quickly as they could, blocking out the aches and pains and praying their legs would carry them a little further.

Jake afforded himself a quiet smile. They'd survived, just, and they had what they needed safely stored on Amy's phone.

CHAPTER 28: SUPPER

As they turned the corner the sun crept down behind the wooden building, filling the sky with oranges and pinks.

Jake wondered what the time was. He'd been trying to work it out but had no idea. Judging by when the sun had set the night before he guessed it must be around seven or eight in the evening.

No wonder we're fucked, he thought, trying to look for signs above the buildings, to see if any of them indicated a restaurant.

He spotted a white board outside a large pale green and white wooden building with white fencing around it and palm trees either side and headed towards it. It was what he'd hoped—a menu board. Jake looked up and read, in very faded pastel red writing, 'Bar & Grill.'

He didn't need to tell the others, he just beelined straight for the place, and they followed instinctively.

The restaurant had at least twenty seats laid up on a terrace area outside, all of which were empty.

"Maybe they're expecting an evening rush," Issy said under her breath as they walked in and sat down at the far end of the terrace.

"I'll go see if someone is around," Jake said, dropping the bag on his chair.

Amy looked at the wooden trellis around her, and the creepers winding their way in and out of the small square holes. It was incredibly humid and there was little breeze. She wondered if it was because they had come further inland that it felt much more sticky and oppressive, or if another storm was on its way. She really hoped it wasn't.

Jake returned from the entrance to the restaurant with a small, round woman, who looked like she was in her fifties, in tow.

Issy thought she would have been pleased to have four customers during what was clearly a quiet spell, but she looked far from it; she looked troubled.

Jake moved the bag and took his seat.

The Bajan woman looked at each of them, lingering her stare on each of them without saying a word, then bustling between them to make up their cutlery and put a menu in front of them.

After a lot of faff she bustled off, and facing away from them, she yelled something that none of them quite caught. It was short and sounded like a command.

Moments later a man appeared from the doorway and strode over to their table. He was tall, around Billy's height, and broad. He looked imposing and serious, and also a little anxious.

"You want something to drink?"

Despite his enormity in size in comparison to the woman, Amy thought the man was very similar. His expressions and his eyes matched hers, and Amy was sure they must be related. He kept shifting his gaze from each of them, and then out to the road beyond the terrace.

Had they not been so desperate for water they may have paid more attention to the oddities of the place. Something was off. Amy didn't care if the man returned shirtless with a bloody knife in his hand, as long as he had a jug of water with him.

"Can we please get some water? And, if we could have that straight away. I'm so thirsty, it's hot out here, you know?" Amy said, trying to sound casual and failing.

The man looked at her, then flitted between each of them again as if searching for something. He nodded and marched away to get their water.

The man was some time, and Jake was just about to go and get the water himself when he reappeared.

Jake all but snatched it out of his hand, forced himself to pour for the others first, then filled his glass and gulped it down in one.

The man's eyes widened, as he watched intently, not saying a word.

Jake shared out the remainder of the jug and necked that too. He looked at the other glasses on the table—all empty.

"Could we please get another?" Amy said as sweetly as she could, worrying this man would think they were animals and throw them out before they could get food.

"And then we're ready to order some food," Issy added.

He paused, nodded, and turned to walk back inside. On his way to the door, Issy, who was in the furthest chair from the door facing across the terrace, saw him glance twice at the road.

"What does he keep looking at?" she asked, straining her eyes but seeing nothing except pastel houses and porches.

It was the strangest town she'd ever seen.

It was cute in its composition, and the colours of the houses, coupled with the incredible colours of the sun-setting sky, made its appearance breathtakingly beautiful. But the emptiness of the place jarred with its visual vibrancy, as it was anything but vibrant where they were.

Aside from their waiter, and the lady who'd greeted them, who they'd agreed was probably his mother, they hadn't seen a soul.

The air was getting thicker too.

"I'm sure there's another storm on the way," Amy said.

Billy looked at the sky. "I think you're right. Look, over there." He pointed at a collection of clouds that looked darker than the rest.

"Looks like it's rolling in off the sea. I'd say we've got another hour or so, then it'll be cats and dogs again."

"Let's eat and see if we can get them to call us a cab. I don't know why but I don't feel like we're particularly welcome here and I don't think we should hang around," said Jake.

"Agreed," Amy said. Issy and Billy nodding.

The man returned with their second jug of water. Having seen how they'd demolished the last jug he hadn't bothered with ice or lemon this time.

"You ready to order?" His voice was deep, and he spoke quietly.

Jake relayed off two of almost everything on the menu. Jerk chicken, ribs, fish, lamb stew, rice and peas, Bajan sweet bread, and four beers.

"I think that should do it." He smiled at the waiter, returning his menu.

The man ignored his smile and finished writing everything down. Then he quickly collected the menus, almost snatching them up, and strode back inside, presumably to relay the order to whoever was cooking.

"Well, it's not exactly the most welcoming place I've ever been but man I'm glad to be here. Thanks for… you know, dragging my ass out of there. I'd be a goner without you," Billy said, as he looked at each of them.

The man, who'd been slow with the service up until now, returned promptly with their beers, ripping the tops off with his bottle opener in front of them, then almost running back inside.

"Anyway." Billy raised his eyebrows and shook his head. "Just wanted to say thanks. Some of you may have tied me up and robbed me, but I still wouldn't want to be here with anyone else." He laughed and made a point of looking at Amy when he emphasized the 'anyone.'

The others laughed and Amy kicked him, embarrassed but delighted to take the olive branch.

"Here's to surviving… and beer!" Jake said raising his bottle. They all clinked their bottles and enjoyed the sensation of the cold, gassy liquid hitting their throats.

"Oh my fucking God that tastes good," Jake said, closing his eyes and properly relaxing his muscles for the first time in what felt like a lifetime.

"Maybe this place isn't so bad."

They sat enjoying the numbing sensation as the alcohol hit their blood streams.

"Storm's definitely coming," said Billy. "Look how much those clouds have moved this way in the last ten minutes."

They all looked at the darkening sky where he was pointing and were surprised to see the dramatic shift in their location and appearance. Not only were they much closer but they were dark black now, whereas they'd been a dirty grey only minutes earlier.

"We're going to lose the sun soon too. When he brings the food, remind me to ask him to call a taxi, or we can. Amy do you still have battery left?"

She reached for her phone and turned it on. "It's at seventeen percent, we're good," she said.

"Okay let's see if they know a local taxi to here first, and if he looks blank at us then maybe we can just get a number. Still no signal?"

"Nope, no idea what's wrong with it."

Issy ran her gaze along the length of the street they were on, peeking through the foliage clinging to the trellis next to her.

It looked like the buildings, all neatly in a row, were houses, but she couldn't see any shops, and they all had porches with no one on them. Some of them had swinging two-seater chairs, which creeped her out. She swore she could hear one of the damn things creaking slightly as it was getting blown backwards and forward. The wind was picking up too. No doubt about the storm now.

"Jake, can you go and see what's taking them so long, please? I would go but it's harder to get out," Issy asked.

"No worries. Yeh, it's getting silly now they've been ages. And this storm's almost on us—we need to find some proper shelter. I have a horrible feeling we're going to get stuck in this place."

His words hung in the air and the looks on Issy, Billy, and Amy's faces made it clear they didn't fancy that much either.

Jake disappeared inside to find out where their food was.

The interior to the restaurant was in almost complete darkness, with only a few dim lamps dotted around. The indoor restaurant was larger than the terrace, and probably had around thirty tables—every single one of them empty.

Jake looked around for the kitchen, and not spotting anything immediately, headed towards the back. He noticed the sign for the toilets, and then over to the right another door.

Ah, that must be it, he thought. But before he could take another step forward he felt a strong hand grip his shoulder.

He panicked and spun round to see their waiter towering over him. Now that he was standing next to him, he could see that he was in fact the same height as Billy, but his shoulders and thick neck made him appear much bigger, and in the darkness, far more frightening.

"You should not be here." Was all he said.

Jake stood dumbfounded by the manner in which the man looked put out, and his choice of words.

He had so many questions, including where was their food and why was it taking so long? But something about the man's look forced him to keep them to himself.

"Sorry," Jake whispered, as he edged around the waiter who refused to step out of his way and hurried back to their table.

For the second time that day he was faced with reporting a situation back to his friends, where half of him wanted to hide the whole truth from them.

In any other circumstance, he would have told them exactly what had happened and encouraged everyone to get the fuck out of there as quickly as possible.

But they needed food, and they wouldn't be able to face another thing without it.

Looking ahead, he could see the storm could cause them further difficulties. It wasn't as though there was a taxi rank around here, and the two people working in the restaurant—the only two people they'd seen—weren't exactly helpful.

Hopefully they could, at least, get a number to call. But if they couldn't, they were going to need to explore some more to find a taxi somewhere else, or find someone else who might be able to help them. And that would involve more walking, and there was no way they could do that without food—not when he literally had smelled it a minute ago.

That was the other thing. Maybe the tiredness, trauma, and lack of nutrition was clouding his judgement. So far nothing had actually happened, not really. And he'd smelled the food, hadn't he?

Jake decided not to say anything.

"It's just coming," he said as he sat back at the table, and really hoped it was.

Just then, either because Jake had hurried him along, or because he'd decided he'd had enough of this group and wanted rid of them, their waiter reappeared carrying the first of the dishes.

The food looked, and smelled, incredible.

Jake swallowed down his apprehension, along with the growing saliva in his mouth, and warily passed out the plates that had been left in the middle.

"This is just…" Issy didn't even get close to finishing her sentence, shoving bread, rice and chicken in her mouth all at once.

She wasn't the only one. The sights and smells of the food were too much for each of them and they ate like ravenous animals, ripping into meat and bread, devouring the food on the table.

"Can we get four more beers?" Billy asked, spotting the man just standing on the steps of the entrance, staring intently out at the road.

The waiter cast Billy a glance, which he couldn't read. He sensed it was annoyance or frustration but didn't dwell on it too long. The food and beer was kicking in, and in that moment, he couldn't have been any more content.

CHAPTER 29: THE WATCHMAN

As he disappeared inside the dark restaurant, they saw the first enormous drops of rain fall on the road. They were so big they burst into smaller droplets on impact, widening their radius and soaking everything they could reach.

Within seconds the sky had opened up, and hard, heavy, fierce rain was shooting down to earth. Small rivers had formed at the sides of the roads, and waterfalls appeared within minutes running off of rooftops.

Thankfully the four of them had largely finished eating. They'd shovelled the selection of food down so quickly they were able to move all of the plates and bowls to the drier side of the table to avoid the splashes. Issy also scooted her chair round to stop herself from getting soaked as the rain jumped through the gaps in the trellis.

"And I thought it got bad in Bristol," Jake said, marvelling at the force of the water falling.

A bolt of lightning lit up the road in front of them, making Issy jump.

"I can't stand those empty porches." She smiled shakily. "They creep me out."

"So, what do we do now?"

"We can try and order the cab now? I'm not sure what state the roads are going to be like though, in this," said Billy.

They looked over towards the doorway and realised the waiter was on the steps, again, looking out across the road. He was mostly covered by the trellis above him, which was thick with plants, but water was still finding a way through, not that he seemed to notice though.

"Excuse me?" Billy asked loudly, trying to get his attention.

There was no response. The man looked like he was miles away. Billy said it louder, almost shouting this time, and it shook the man from his reverie.

"Could we get the check, another round of beers, and can we order a cab?"

The man looked at Billy, nodded, and returned inside.

"He doesn't say much, does he?" Amy said.

"What's that?" Issy had been looking to see where the waiter's focus had been, and she was now staring intently in the same direction across the road.

It was almost dark now and difficult to see. There was one streetlight and the lamps from the restaurant offered a small glow from their side of the road.

The other side was mostly in darkness. A few flickering lights had come on inside some of the homes, showing them they were not completely alone, and the houses were inhabited, at least some of them were.

But Issy was staring at one particular house almost opposite to them. She'd remembered it from when they first sat down because it was the one that creeped her out the most.

The wooden walls were painted a pastel red that was faded and in disrepair. The windows and shutters were white and had one of the swinging porch chairs she hated so much. It must have been positioned in a part of the street that got the most wind coming through because it had been swinging more noticeably than any of the others since they'd arrived.

Now she was staring at it, forcing herself not to blink, so that when the lightning next struck she could confirm what she'd seen hadn't been imagined.

The others had stopped talking and could see what she was doing. They too stared hard in the direction her head was turned. She was so taught and focused, they knew better than to interrupt with questions.

Issy didn't have to wait long. A thin jagged streak of lightning cut across the sky directly over the house they were looking at, illuminating the porch for a brief couple of seconds, as if someone had shone a giant searchlight on it.

"Did you see that?" She turned to them, fear in her voice. The others nodded grimly.

Standing next to the now wildly swinging porch seat was a black figure. He had a wide brim hat on, long hair, and a long dark coat. Now the light had gone, that was all they could make out in the gloom, but when the lightning had struck they could all clearly see the man was staring at them. They couldn't see his expression or make out his features, but they knew it was them he was looking at.

"Who the hell is that?" Amy asked, her voice a frightened whisper.

"I don't know. Probably just a local giving us the eye because we're not from round here. But keep an eye on him," Jake whispered loud enough for just them to hear, as he stood up to go inside.

"Where are you going?" hissed Issy, not wanting him to leave them at the table.

"I'm going to get that taxi number so we can get the fuck out of here. I'd rather face the roads than that crazy across the street, who's decided he doesn't like the look of us."

Jake had an urge to crouch down as he went across the terrace to the entrance so the man across the street wouldn't see him but told himself to stop being stupid and forced himself to walk tall. He couldn't prevent his heart from beating faster though and could feel fear creeping up on him.

The waiter was lurking just inside the door and Jake almost walked in to him.

"Oh, hi. Could we get a taxi now? Or if you just have a number that you can give to us and we can call one? It's just that, we're in a bit of a hurry," he stated, when the waiter didn't move.

Finally, the man looked at him tearing his gaze away from across the street. This time Jake knew what he was looking at.

"You can't leave, not now," he said quietly, then returned his look to across the street.

"What… what do you mean we can't leave?" Jake was taken aback.

"That man. You've seen him, and he's seen you. If you tried to leave now—it would be very bad."

"I don't know what the fuck you're talking about," Jake said sternly, feeling a cold chill running up his spine. "But we'll leave whenever we want." He turned and hurried back down the steps before the man could say anything else.

The waiter had scared Jake, but he could sense the waiter's fear too. He didn't fully understand what was going on but knew the threat from across the street was real and didn't plan to hang about and find out just how real it was going to get.

He splashed down the steps and practically ran back to the table.

"Is that bloke still across the street? Has he moved?" he asked urgently.

"No, I've been watching him watching us. This is horrible. What happened inside?" Issy replied.

"I'm not sure exactly. The waiter said we can't leave, I don't know if he was warning us or threatening us, either way I think we need to get the fuck out of here."

Issy, who'd turned to look at Jake's face when he'd been talking, quickly turned her head back to the direction it had been facing and tried to find the dark figure on the porch.

"Fuck! Oh, fuck. Where are you? He's gone, I can't see him anymore what if… wait…" Issy was straining, trying to make her eyes see better in the gloomy street now only illuminated by the odd streetlight, house lamp, bolt of lightning, and very occasionally, when there was a break in the storm clouds, the moon, which was now out.

She'd lost the figure from the side of the swing-seat, but she now thought she saw him leaning on the porch balcony, smoking.

"I can see him again, but I'm scared. I think Jake's right, this guy could be a complete psycho. He's been staring at us for ages and now the waiter's warning us about him—let's get out of here."

They signalled their agreement by getting to their feet. Jake gathered up the yellow bag, and Billy took out a load of Barbados dollars and left them on the table.

If the waiter had been warning them, he felt bad eating so much and not paying, plus he didn't want to give anyone else any reason to chase them. There was plenty of that going around as it was.

Issy hadn't moved. She was mesmerised by the end of the man's cigarette, which glowed bright red every time he took a drag. Somehow, she knew that as soon as he'd finished, as soon as he'd taken the last suck and the end burned brightly for the last time, they would be out of time and he'd come for them. She knew that, and that's what made her freeze with fear.

"Come on, Issy, now!" Amy demanded, pulling on her arm to get her to move.

The others were ready, and as soon as Issy got up and was with them, they turned and fled to the end of the terrace—where they found the big waiter standing in their way.

Jake was just wondering whether to drop his shoulder and try to run and smash the guy out of the way, when the waiter surprised him.

"Please, this way," he said, pointing inside the restaurant.

His words, and anxious demeanour caused Jake and the others to freeze. "He's coming," Issy whisper-yelled.

Jake quickly glanced across to his right and wondered whether the creature from the sea had managed to turn itself into human form because the man walking towards them was every bit as monstrous.

They could see now in the streetlight his hair was even longer than they'd thought, it swirled wildly in the storm around his face and shoulders. It was dark grey not black, as was his thick, matted beard. His hat was pulled low over his forehead to keep out the rain, but Jake thought he caught a glimpse of his dark, dead eyes. His long, leather coat was soaking wet, with water streaming off him, and his black boots caused water to spray across the road with every step, making it look like he was gliding on water towards them.

"This way," the waiter said again, with more urgency this time.

Now there was no decision to be made. Jake didn't fully understand what was going on, or what role this man or his mother had to play in it, but he was certain that the man was trying to help them, and he turned to tell the others to go on through.

Jake waited until Issy had dashed past him and in to the dark restaurant before he took a quick look to his right to see how much of a head start they had. The man was in the middle of the road and still coming, his hands were by his sides and he didn't look like he was coming to talk.

Jake turned his head away and ran inside after the others.

CHAPTER 30: RUN

It took a few seconds for Jake's eyes to accustom to the gloomy restaurant lighting, but he pushed forward driving his friends on before he could fully see.

He'd glimpsed the man's face from halfway across the road and that was enough to scare the life out of him, he didn't need to see it any closer.

A loud crack and someone screamed up ahead. Another few hurried steps and Jake found Amy on the ground clutching her leg. She'd clattered in to a table and tumbled to the floor. Issy and Billy swiftly reached down to pick her up, ignoring the grimace on her face and hauling Amy to her feet.

While they were helping her up Jake turned to find their pursuer and see how far away he was now.

"RUN!" he screamed.

Jake saw the man with the grey beard release his grip on their waiter's throat, and his body slump to the ground in the doorway. The man looked down to make sure the waiter wasn't getting back up. He was still breathing but even Jake could see the fear in his eyes from where he was and knew the waiter had absolutely no intention of moving.

Having made the same assessment, the dark figure stepped over the waiter's paralysed body and in to the restaurant, looking for them.

Amy had heard Jake's shocking scream and froze. Issy, who'd spotted the back door, grabbed her arm and pulled her in the direction of the exit. Amy sprang to life and they both sprinted towards it, Jake and Billy running after them, straining every muscle to get there before they were caught and dragged back inside.

They reached the door and burst through, hearing something break and splinter. The door was most likely locked, but fear was propelling them forward. They half fell out in to the humid, wet night, the rain still falling hard and soaking each of them through in a matter of seconds.

They kept running, and running, hitting dense jungle similar to their surroundings on the trail on the way up.

Smashing through branches, tripping over roots and picking themselves out of the mud, they didn't stop until Jake found a cluster of trees with leaves and vines draping down over its exterior. It looked like a den he'd played hide and seek in when he was a kid. He grabbed Issy and Amy and pulled them inside, Billy catching on and jumping in after them.

Despite desperately needing to catch their breath they each tried to stop breathing, listening hard for the sound of footsteps above the rain and their hammering hearts.

They waited, listening. Nothing.

The rain crept slowly down dripping from leaf to leaf and eventually soaking the ground. Despite their discomfort, none of them made a sound.

They weren't sure how long they remained in that position. Jake couldn't tell if they'd been there ten minutes or half an hour, his sole focus had been on escaping then locating their pursuer. They kept listening intently, expecting to hear footsteps, but the only noise they heard was the rain finding its way through the forest, showing no sign of stopping. It was relentless.

Jake looked at Issy, who was directly next to him then craned his neck to make eye contact with Amy and Billy, to signal it was time to make a run for it.

But before he could convey his message, they heard something snap.

In the wet and the rain they were letting some noises go. The crashing of branches underneath the weight of the water, or the surprisingly heavy thud of each droplet as it hit the ground. But the snap of the branch was too crisp, too clear, and none of them could imagine anything else had caused it but the dark figure with the grey beard who seemed intent on catching them.

Instantly, all thoughts of moving were abandoned, and they froze where they were.

Nothing.

Another ten minutes went by and Jake mustered up the courage to look out of their sanctuary to see if there was any sign of their pursuer, or if the snap had been a sign he'd come close but failed to find their hiding place and moved on.

He edged his way to the edge of the den and slowly poked his head out of the bottom, looking left then right.

Rain poured down on Jake's forehead, dripping over his eyes and mouth, making it difficult for him to see.

Eventually he was satisfied that either the man had come and gone, or that he wasn't going to make a move until they fully revealed themselves, and he was actually lying in wait somewhere. He very much hoped it was the former.

Jake signalled the others to move, slowly, and crept, hardly breathing, out of their hiding hole.

"Has he gone?" Amy asked, petrified the man would appear from out of the darkness, striding at them.

"Yes, he's gone," Jake lied, with no intention of telling them his real suspicion, that the man with the beard was actually camouflaged and lying in wait somewhere deep in the forest waiting for them to reveal themselves.

"Okay. Let's go," Issy said.

Jake suspected she had the same concerns and had come to the same conclusion—they had to keep moving. They had no choice.

One by one they left their hideout.

A river was forming, running through the centre of the forest because of all the rain.

"It's got to come out somewhere," Jake said, leading them down next to it.

Billy was bringing up the rear and was still slowest in their group, he couldn't help frequently glancing behind him for fear he'd get grabbed out of the darkness.

"Come on, Billy," Jake hissed, after Issy informed him there was a gap developing, and worried they were leaving him behind.

Billy nodded and doubled his efforts, slipping at one point but pride getting him quickly to his feet.

Eventually, up ahead, Jake spotted a clearing in the trees.

He wasn't sure until he saw the headlights of a car cut through the forest that it was a road they had come across, but now there was no mistake.

"Come on!" He turned and yelled to his friends, worried they'd been tracked this far, and were about to be ambushed. Now was the time to make a run for it.

But there was no ambush. The only sound they heard in the forest was the water unrepentantly finding its way past every obstacle to the ground. Soaking it further.

More headlights.

Jake led the way to the end of the forest path and poked his head out of the clearing.

He looked left and could see the road winding away, with nothing populating its sides other than palm trees and shrubs.

To his right, more of the same, with a few more pastel-coloured houses in the distance.

He pulled his head back in to relay what he'd seen to the others.

"We've got two options. We can go back and try to find another route through this forest, hope we hit another town—a normal town, where we might actually find some help, or we follow the road and try to hitchhike back to our resort. I'm sure that way is south so at least we'd be heading in the right direction."

"I'm not going back in the forest," Amy said stubbornly, her eyes still wide with fear. "He's still in there, I know it. At least on the road there'll be other cars, houses, people who will see if…" She couldn't say the words.

Billy and Issy agreed. They waited a couple more minutes to catch their breath then filed out on to the road, heading south.

Issy took up her position at the back of the group and stuck out her thumb at the first sound of an approaching car.

Two old bangers rattled past without stopping before the third, after they'd been walking for just over ten minutes, stopped for them. It was an old, white, four-door Toyota. Its flanks covered in muddy spray.

The door flung open and before they had a chance to speak, the driver leaned up out of the driver side window, holding on to the frame, poking his head over the top. "Get in," he told them.

The driver was a young guy in his early to mid-twenties they guessed, around the same age as them. Although he was maybe five to eight years younger than their waiter from the restaurant, he carried with him the same anxious mannerisms.

Jake looked at the others to try and gauge their thoughts on what to do.

"The waiter tried to help us. I think we should go with this guy. I think he's trying to help us escape too, and the alternative is we keep walking and that man in there…" Jake's voice trailed off.

They all nodded.

"I'm the biggest, I'll go in the front. You guys get in the back," Billy said.

They all got in the car cautiously, while the young Bajan nervously tapped his index finger on the steering wheel.

As soon as they were in he put his foot on the accelerator and sped off.

Either they were putting significant distance between themselves and danger with every passing moment, or they'd just sat themselves in an even more perilous position with no easy way of escape.

Jake anxiously looked out of the rear window to see if there was any sign of a last minute attack. As the trees turned into a blur, and the car followed the winding road around the island, he was satisfied there wasn't—and turned his attention to their driver.

CHAPTER 31: TAXI DRIVER

Amy flattened her hair down, so it dropped against the side of her face. She was anxious. She looked at the young driver in the front seat and wondered if he was actually taking them back to their holiday resort, or to some new hellish ordeal.

"How long have you lived on the island?" Billy tried to make conversion.

No reply.

The driver was fully focused on the road ahead. Almost fully focused, except every few minutes he looked in his mirrors, nearly expecting their pursuer to appear out of nowhere and haul the car to a halt.

After twenty minutes or so the driver finally spoke, making them jump. "It's not safe," he said simply, as if that was explanation enough.

After a long pause, with no follow up, Billy asked what he meant.

No reply. The driver acted like he'd never said anything and tightened his grip on the steering wheel.

Sensing nothing more was to be gained, they decided not to press him further.

Eventually they approached a street they recognised, and Jake jumped to attention, relieved they were nearly free of this unbearable taxi.

The driver pulled up at the back of the resort and turned on the light in the front of the car.

"You need to leave," he said.

"How much do we owe you?" Billy asked, desperate to get out and join the others who'd already jumped out the back.

The driver stared at him, his eyes conveying sadness and fear.

"Hear me when I speak. You need to leave. It is no longer safe for you here."

Billy stared dumbfounded, unsure what to say or do next.

Finally, he reached for his wallet, retrieved fifty dollars and got out of the car, leaving the money on the seat before he shut the door.

The four of them hurried along the driveway to the resort, glancing over their shoulders for some final surprise, but none came.

The lights of the cab shone on them for a split-second before it drove away, and they were finally able to relax.

CHAPTER 32: DECISION

Amy woke to the sun bursting through the shutters in her room.

She had no idea how long she'd been asleep, and when the memories of the last few days flooded her mind, she questioned if any of it was real.

She glanced across the room and saw her green dress on the floor. She could see the blood stains confirming every nightmarish vision was a reality she had lived through.

"I'm still alive," she mumbled, taking some solace in that fact.

She looked for Issy and found her fast asleep in her bed not far away.

Seeing her friend alive and well too, her heart lifted.

Amy swung her feet around in the bed, so they were free from the covers, and planted them on the cold marble floor.

She stood up gingerly, and slowly walked to the big French doors.

They'd forgotten to draw the shutters before they'd passed out, so she could see the sea without any obstacle. Today, without a storm cloud in sight and the sun shining brightly, if looked inviting and friendly.

"Asshole," she uttered at the vast expanse of water. Issy stirred awake.

Amy watched her as she opened her eyes. They widened and filled with terror as Issy went through the same process as Amy had when she'd woken up.

Amy went over to calm her friend. "It's okay. It's over," she said.

Issy thought about asking questions, a million of them, for reassurance. Hoping her friend would tell her it had all been a bad dream. But she knew better and hardened her heart.

"What do we do now?" she asked.

Amy opened her mouth to answer, then paused. She held her breath thinking about what to say.

After a long pause she said, "I'm not going back. Not until we've found it."

Issy looked at Amy, unsurprised.

"Me neither," she replied, managing a smile.

"Okay then. Let's go and see those two idiots and make sure they're not going to flake on us." She laughed, finally letting go.

They got dressed quickly and headed down the paved path to the boys' apartments, arriving at Billy's first.

Amy knocked loudly.

"Just a minute," Billy shouted from inside.

They heard him stumbling around. The door opened and Billy stood bleary-eyed and bare-chested in front of them.

Amy noticed his wounds had been cleaned up but guessed they were going to leave a scar. She also noticed Billy had lost weight, even in the short time they'd been here.

"Come on, we're going to get breakfast," she said, looking at her watch. "Actually, not breakfast, not even brunch… fuck, it's three in the afternoon. We were asleep for ages! Anyway, we're going to get food. All of us. I'm calling a group meeting."

Billy looked at her and grinned.

"Okay, sure. Give me two minutes to freshen up and put some clothes on—does Jake know?"

"Not yet, we're on our way to his place next. We'll go get him and meet you at the main restaurant in fifteen minutes."

Amy didn't wait for a reply. She turned away and marched off towards Jake's apartment, her skirt swaying from side to side with each forceful stride.

Issy shrugged her shoulders and smiled at Billy.

"See you in a bit," she said, turning away and catching up with her friend.

Jake was fully clothed and bright-eyed when he opened his door and looked like he'd been awake for a while. He had the same glint in his eye that Amy did. The treasure was occupying his thoughts, and the memories of all they'd survived were, to him, a sign they were on the right path, and should absolutely keep going.

"How are you feeling?" he asked them both, first looking for Amy's injury to inspect it then looking them in the eyes to check for signs of fatigue, or worse, loss of appetite for the prize.

Jake had been going over their next moves in his head, pacing in his apartment for the last few hours, and analysing everything they'd been through to see if they could have done things differently.

One thing he was certain of, he couldn't have come this far on his own. He needed the others if he was going to find whatever was to be found, and he also didn't want to have to try and go the rest of the way on his own. Or even just him and Billy. Everything they'd been through made him feel like he'd known the girls a lot longer than he had, and the four of them just worked.

"So, what's the plan?" he asked, satisfied they hadn't come to tell him they were too traumatised to stay, and were getting the next flight home.

"I'm calling a group meeting. Main restaurant. Ten minutes," Amy said, smiling.

"Fair enough. I'll grab my wallet and meet you there."

Jake turned back in to the apartment, located his wallet on the nightstand, and sat down for a moment.

He stared out of the window at the swaying palm trees and the water beyond and savoured the moment.

"No going back now."

CHAPTER 33: HORIZON

Billy hacked at his pancakes hungrily. The cooked blueberries dripped from his fork as he shovelled food in his mouth.

"But, why the fuck did they help us?" Billy asked.

"I don't know. We don't know that they definitely did, but it felt that way. The waiter could have warned us, and he didn't, but we saw him try to stand up to that man. And the taxi driver seemed like he was part of it. He warned us. I don't get how they knew each other, or what had happened, but he knew," Amy added.

"So, let me get this right…" Jake began, trying to conclude the last hour's discussion. "We drank the rum, it drove you to find the first compass, it somehow awakened a killer tiger shark and a grey-haired psychopath hell-bent on killing us, but a village full of in-the-know locals tried to help us? Just sounds fucking crazy."

"I swear something took hold of me. It wanted me to find the compass," Amy jumped back in, getting frustrated. "But the shark and the man wanted to stop us. As for the villagers or whoever, I don't know if they wanted to stop us, help us, or if they were just caught in the middle."

"All I know is, we are on to something, and we need to keep going," Billy said and stuffed the last of a pancake in his mouth.

They struggled to agree on what had actually happened to them, but there was no doubting their desire to carry on and see what they could find in Antigua.

"So, it's settled then," Amy said. "We'll check out early and head to the airport tomorrow."

A Few Words

Thank you for reading. I hope you enjoyed it! It would be greatly appreciated if you could leave a short, honest review on the site you purchased this book.

Book 2, The Antigua Trail, and book 3, Caribbean Ghosts, are both now available on Amazon.

For more Caribbean adventures and news of upcoming novels, follow me on Instagram @jwilliamauthor

Printed in Great Britain
by Amazon